Her Mistletoe Husband
Renee Roszel

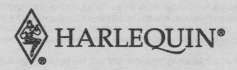

HARLEQUIN®

TORONTO • NEW YORK • LONDON
AMSTERDAM • PARIS • SYDNEY • HAMBURG
STOCKHOLM • ATHENS • TOKYO • MILAN • MADRID
PRAGUE • WARSAW • BUDAPEST • AUCKLAND

To my real-life sisters,
Norda and Ronda.
Can you find yourselves among the three
Crosby sisters?

ISBN 0-373-03528-4

HER MISTLETOE HUSBAND

First North American Publication 1998.

"You're a challenge, Miss Crosby."

She eyed him with skepticism. Something seemed to dawn on her, and her green eyes went appealingly wide. "What do you think you're going to do? Seduce me?"

"Yes," he whispered.

She flinched and he experienced a twinge of compassion. He didn't like putting her out of her home. But she would be okay. Elissa Crosby had more backbone than any ten women he knew.

As they swayed intimately on the dance floor, he could feel her slim body move subtly against his. He found himself growing more and more aroused by her reluctant nearness. Lord, she was a temptress, even when temptation was the last thing on her mind.

Damn the woman! If she would only throw herself at him, he'd grow bored and lose interest. He gazed into those sexy, guarded eyes again, his lips quirking in self-mockery. *Like hell he would*. Bowing his head, he lowered his face toward hers.

Enchanted Brides

The Myth

The stately D'Amour mansion stands majestically in the countryside, its absentee owner rumored to be living in Europe. Closed for years, this mansion has a charming myth surrounding it. Legend says that the mansion is enchanted and that "an unmarried woman who sleeps within its walls on her birthday, when the moon is full, will marry the first man she sees in the morning."

Her Mistletoe Husband is the third in Renee Roszel's spellbinding **Enchanted Brides** trilogy.

Also in the **Enchanted Brides** trilogy:
To Marry a Stranger (#3470)
Married By Mistake! (#3488)

Praise for the trilogy:

"Renee Roszel delivers a fast-paced, humorous tale as she blends commanding characters with a strong premise and lovable secondary characters in Her Mistletoe Husband."
—Romantic Times

"Ms. Roszel adds sound characterization to a touching premise to win our hearts."
—Romantic Times on To Marry a Stranger

CHAPTER ONE

ELISSA'S elbow hit the floor with a thump, waking her and making her wince. She groaned, but as soon as the sound was out of her mouth, she clamped her hand over her lips.

What if *he* heard?

A shiver raked her body, but the reaction had more to do with her terror than the cold. She blinked, clearing away the blur of sleep. It was dark, very dark, except for the slash of light at the bottom of the door to the closet where she was hiding. She couldn't believe she'd fallen asleep, but even in her fright exhaustion had finally taken its toll.

The slash of light at the bottom of the door!

She realized it must be after dawn. Around midnight she'd scrambled into the deserted D'Amour mansion through a loose board nailed over a window. She'd been sure the man following her hadn't seen where she'd entered, but just to be safe, she'd hidden in this upstairs closet, barely breathing. For hours. Then she'd fallen into a fitful sleep.

Her whole body ached and felt cramped. It was so cold. Of course, being December, that shouldn't be a surprise. Still, Elissa wasn't accustomed to sleeping in closets in abandoned, unheated mansions. Stiff from the cold and the cramped position she'd been curled in, she shifted her wristwatch into the light stream. Seven o'clock! She couldn't believe it.

What a lousy way to begin a birthday. First the flat

tire, then, when she'd realized the flat *was* her spare, and started to walk home, there had been movement in the brush. *A man.* A big man. Something had glinted in the light of the full moon as he'd skulked from bush to bush—a wristwatch? A belt buckle? The blade of an ax? Her survival instincts had gone into high gear, especially after the unsigned letter she received last week. Threatening and scary. The police had taken a report and said they'd look into it. Even so, the sergeant had tried to reassure her, explaining it was most likely a prank, nothing to be worried about.

Nothing! Well, she'd like to know what they'd think now, after she'd been forced to huddle in a closet all night. She stood, swallowing to bolster her courage, assuring herself that not even a certified nutcase would hang around in subfreezing temperatures all night. Taking a deep breath she cracked open the door and peered into the bare room. Cobwebs, dust motes and the smell of must were her only companions. Sunlight streamed in the dingy arched windows, the brightness of the day strengthening her resolve. Stalkers belonged to the night, didn't they?

As she emerged from the closet, the creak of the door sent a tingle of apprehension along her spine, but she controlled her reaction. "Elissa, are you a man or are you a mouse?" she muttered, then shook her head, her lips quirking. "Okay, so you're neither. Just *go.*"

As soundlessly as she could, in a mansion that seemed to squawk and groan with every step, as if it were a cantankerous old grump, she made her way down the grand staircase and along the dark hall to the den. After peering out of the window through which she'd entered, she determined that no large men with hatchets were lurking nearby. With a prayer on her lips, she slipped outside, not the easiest thing to do in her tweed suit's slender skirt.

From her vantage point at the side of the house, she could see her old sedan, a hundred yards down the road, but she couldn't see the front of the mansion. She hugged herself, watching her breath frost the air. What was she to do? Getting back to her inn and to a telephone was high on her list—just below staying alive. The trip would be cut in half if she took the shortcut through the woods. With a determined nod, she pivoted toward the back of the manor.

As she rounded the corner, a massive male figure loomed. "Oh, my Lord!" she cried. *He was still here!* Reacting on instinct, the self-defense course she'd taken flashed through her mind. She clawed at the stranger's face and shot her knee up, finding her target. "Take that you pervert!" she yelled.

The intruder groaned then doubled over, and she knew she'd debilitated him enough to make her escape. She lurched away, scrambling into the woods. Stumbling and tripping along the rocky path, she cursed her unsuitable pumps. Her lungs burned with the cold, her brain whirring as she cast around in her memory. Who was that man? She only got a glimpse of him, but he seemed too well dressed to have been slinking around in the woods all night. And, unless he'd taken an advanced course in personal hygiene, he didn't resemble any of her down-and-out law clients. She had a feeling she would have remembered those extraordinary eyes—the color of silver lightning—even squinting in pain and shock.

As she reached the back steps of her inn, she paused to get her breath. Sucking in gasps of stinging air, she decided it didn't matter if she recalled him or not. He had to be someone from her time as a Kansas City lawyer. She'd only practiced for four years, and that seemed like an eternity ago. But apparently she wasn't forgotten. Somebody with a very big grudge remembered her.

She hugged herself, stifling another shiver and exhaled a frosty cloud. The most important thing at the moment was, she'd gotten away. Sinking to the lowest step, she pushed a shaky hand through her fiery curls. She was baffled. Had this man blamed her for losing his case and for his being sent to prison? Or was he possibly the relative of some victim who felt that her defense had set a guilty man free? If that were the case, then why had he waited years after she'd given up the practice of law to come after her? Her move from Kansas City had been no secret. Whoever he was, she hoped a knee to the groin was enough to make him change his mind about coming after her.

Unfortunately she had her doubts. "Who are you, mister?" she mused in a winded exhale. "What do you want with me?"

Elissa felt better with the attention of the two young patrolmen who had answered her call. They'd checked around the D'Amour mansion and searched the woods between the estate and her inn. They'd even taken her tire into town and gotten it patched and returned her car to her. She loved small towns. You wouldn't catch a Kansas City cop doing that.

The two officers promised to increase their patrols in the area and took down her sketchy description of the man she'd kneed that morning. One of the cops, built like a professional football player, startled her by asking her out to dinner. She was working on a nice way to decline and still get her extra night patrol when the front door of the inn opened.

She looked up to see at a towering man backlit by afternoon brightness. Dressed in an impeccable suit he seemed to completely block her door. He was handsome, his chiseled features marred only by three scratches along his jaw. When he met her gaze, she saw a flash of silver lighting in his eyes, and she screamed.

Plucking up the letter opener from the reception desk, she brandished it in his direction. "That's the pervert who attacked me this morning! *Get* him!"

At that moment a second man slipped inside the door. Elissa recognized him as a detective in the Branson police department. A wiry man with ginger freckles on his balding skull, his name had something to do with food, but she couldn't remember what. She stilled with her weapon thrust forward, making her look like Teddy Roosevelt pointing out the whites of his enemy's eyes.

The tall pervert seemed to register having met her before, too, and those amazing eyes narrowed. "You," he growled.

"Don't just stand there," she shouted, scanning the frozen cops and the detective who stood beside her stalker. "*Grab* him. Throw him to the ground and cuff him. *He attacked me!*"

The tall stranger scowled at her. "I attacked you?"

He took an ominous step toward her, and her ability to move returned. She waved the letter opener menacingly, adding some ad-libbed footwork, as if she were one of the Three Musketeers. "You certainly did attack me!" She eyed the cops with a pleading expression. "He's dangerous, I tell you?"

"Me?" The stranger's lips curled in a mocking smile. "Who was the one who ended up in a heap on the ground?"

The cop who had asked her to dinner took a step toward the tall man, but the detective waved him off.

"Why isn't anybody arresting that psychopath? Don't let him come near me!"

The scowling stranger touched his damaged cheek. "Miss, I wouldn't come near you unless you were declawed and your feet were glued to the floor."

"Elissa," the detective broke in, moving forward and extending his hand. "I'm Sergeant Jerry Hamm."

"I remember you, Sergeant." She tried to smile but her emotions were too wrought up for pleasantries. "And your wife. Minny, I think?"

"Right." The sergeant had a quiet, oval face, his features almost delicate. He smiled encouragingly, showing off small, straight teeth. When she didn't relinquish her letter opener to take his hand, he dropped his arm to his side. "Anyway, this is Alex D'Amour. He owns the mansion, er, next to your property."

Elissa had a protest on the tip of her tongue, but the sergeant's words stopped her. Her mouth worked for several seconds before she could speak. "This—this man *owns* the D'Amour mansion?"

Sergeant Hamm nodded. "I'm afraid we're here with bad news."

She frowned, her gaze shifting from the sergeant to the tall, immaculately dressed interloper with her fingernail marks on his face. "Then you didn't follow me last night when my car broke down, and stalk me outside the mansion all night, and when I came out you didn't try to..." Her question died away as she watched a dark brow lift in incredulity.

Looking at him now, dressed as if he spent more time in boardrooms than insane asylums, the idea that he was her stalker was starting to seem a little crazy. Okay, maybe a *lot* crazy. Perhaps she hadn't been stalked after all. Certainly not by this man. Her mind spun with anxiety and confusion. Was she merely overwrought because of the ominous letter, seeing things that weren't really there?

Doubt settled in her stomach as if it were a hot rock. She could see in the cops' expressions that, with her wild accusations that Mr. D'Amour was her stalker, they'd concluded she was nothing but a flighty female, crying wolf. She had to face the possibility that they might be right.

Trying to regain some of her pride, she straightened her spine. "Well," she said warily, refusing to totally relinquish her suspicions, "just—just because you dress well doesn't mean you wouldn't stalk me."

He inhaled, nostrils flaring in obvious exasperation. "That's generous of you, Miss Crosby. But no thanks."

When he moved toward her, she backed away wielding the letter opener again. "What are you doing?"

He lifted a leather briefcase and laid it on the oak reception desk that separated them. Flicking the latches, he opened it. "As Sergeant Hamm said, I'm bringing bad news."

She eyed him with mistrust, recalling the sergeant had said something like that. Unfortunately she'd been too preoccupied with making an idiot of herself for his words to register. "Bad news?"

He retrieved a file folder and tossed it onto the desktop in front of her. "I recently discovered I'm the heir to the D'Amour mansion, Miss Crosby." He lifted his gaze to meet hers again, dark lashes framing those stunning eyes. His expression was no longer angry, but hardly pleasant. "I also own this inn."

She heard the words but they didn't make sense. She stared at him, bewildered. "What?"

He tapped the folder with one long, tanned finger. "I've brought evidence."

She shook her head, running both hands through her hair as she tried to clear her brain. "But—no. I don't understand. I bought this inn from the caretaker. He'd been left the property in the D'Amour's will."

"I'm sorry, Miss Crosby," Sergeant Hamm said. "I know this is a blow to you, but the man who sold you the inn is a con artist. Extremely good. Fortunately he's in jail now, in Texas, for a similar crime." He indicated the folder before her. "Mr. D'Amour brought you a copy of his arrest record. The jerk fooled a lot of people over the years with scams like this. He found a likely property. Had all the right papers. At least they look right enough to convince the probate court and the title company." He shrugged sloping shoulders. "I'm sorry to be the one to have to tell you."

She stared at the sergeant, her mind numb.

"I understand you're a lawyer so I suggest you read these documents," Mr. D'Amour said. "Once you do, everything will be clear."

When he withdrew his hand from the desk her gaze traveled sluggishly to the yellow folder then rocketed to those silver eyes. "No," she whispered. "There's been some mistake."

He pursed his lips, his brows knitting. Without response, he shook his head.

"I'm so sorry, Elissa," Jerry Hamm said, again, looking contrite. She'd met him and his wife several times at Branson functions, and liked him. She supposed he had to be there, to make it official, and she could tell he was far from pleased with the assignment. The sadness in his brown eyes frightened her more than anything this arrogant stranger had said.

"I know I seem abrupt, Miss Crosby," Mr. D'Amour said, breaking through the tense silence, "But I've given up my legal practice in L.A. and I've decided to live in the Midwest, to turn my grandparents' home into a golf club and lodge. Branson is growing by leaps and bounds, and a resort near the city would be a good investment." He closed his briefcase, snapping it shut with precise movements. All business. "I'm afraid the inn will have to be torn down to make room for the golf course. But you may continue operations through December while you make other living arrangements." He took the briefcase in his hand. "Don't take reservations for after the new year, however. I'll need to take possession then." Scanning the place in a cursory examination, he added more to himself than to her, "It looks quite livable."

She stiffened at the surprise in his tone. "What did you expect?"

His glance returned to her and he shrugged wide shoulders—the image of cold-blooded elegance. "I admit, I didn't expect this. But since it's in such good condition, I'll use it as my operating headquarters while the renovations to my mansion are going on. Now, if you'll show me to a room?"

Elissa stared blankly at the brazen man before her— the man who had, with only a few words, ruined her life.

"We'll be going now," the husky police officers mumbled, shuffling around to go. Before Elissa registered what was happening, both patrolmen and Sergeant Hamm had gone—no doubt along with her extra patrols or any credibility she might have had before she'd accused this well-heeled lawyer of stalking her. She supposed he had every right to be walking on his *own* property.

"Well?" That one word stirred her from her stupor and she glanced up in question. "My room?"

His room? The man had unbelievable gall! She glared at him. He might own the D'Amour mansion, but he did not own her inn! "You can't come in here and take over! *Get out!*" She thrust a stiff arm toward the door.

His jaw worked and her gaze was drawn again to the damage she had done to him. It's a good thing she didn't know then what she knew now, or she might have clawed him to shreds. "I'm afraid you don't have a legal leg to stand on, Miss Crosby," he cautioned. "Don't make things worse." He inclined his head toward the stairs, a clear command to be shown to a room.

She battled an urge to kick him in the shins, but she was afraid she'd just end up seeing Sergeant Hamm again, under less-than-sociable circumstances. Hating the idea that she might have to humor this overbearing man for even a few days, she let her arm fall to her side. She told herself that it would only be until this thing got straightened out, then she could kick him out on his expensively suited backside. "I'm going to fight you on this," she warned.

"Feel free to sue me, Miss Crosby. But, you'll lose." The way he said it, with such cool assurance and total absence of bluster, made her shiver. "My room, Miss Crosby?"

She eyed him contemptuously. She'd be hanged if she was going to give him one of her guest rooms. "We're full," she lied. It wasn't totally untrue. She'd reserved her two best rooms for her sisters and their husbands, who would be arriving in a few days to spend Christmas and New Years.

"This is my inn, remember?" he said. "I could send everybody away if I chose. Think real hard."

Those silver eyes held a determined glint and alarm skittered up her spine. With a mutinous lift of her chin, she said, "You can stay in the basement parlor. The couch folds out."

His expression told her he knew exactly what she was doing, and his brows furrowed at her ploy. "Is there office space down there?"

"*My* office is down there."

He didn't looked thoroughly pleased, but finally nodded. "All right. Until a room becomes available."

She grabbed the folder and pivoted away. "When hell freezes over, buster," she growled under her breath.

"I heard that."

She spun to glower at him. "I'm *thrilled.*"

A mocking brow rose, and Elissa was disappointed to see that her most intimidating glare didn't have him shaking in his expensive wing tips. "Where's the basement, Miss Crosby?"

She marched away from him into the staircase hall, heading toward the kitchen. "It's on the way to hell," she snapped back. "I feel sure you'll find it."

She was startled by the derisive chuckle at her back. *How dare he find entertainment in the annihilation of her life!*

Alex D'Amour didn't know who he was trying to push around. Elissa Crosby was not a woman to easily give up her dreams. The instant she hit the kitchen, she slammed the folder onto the table, startling Bella, the plump cook. Stubby hands fluttered to a ruffly bodice. Elissa looked up and tried to smile. "Sorry. Could you get me a cup of coffee?"

The middle-aged woman nodded and hurried to the pot. The coffee in Elissa's mug had gone cold before she looked up from the documents to take a sip. Making a face, she rubbed her eyes. It looked bad. Mr. D'Amour seemed to have every legal right to the property. But then, the documentation she had looked just as good— and it had passed muster with the probate court and the title company. Even so, the face staring up at her from the police rap sheet looked a little like the man she'd known as the caretaker who'd sold her the old Victorian house. Not exactly like him, but...

And he had been in a hurry to sell, offering her a fantastic deal for cash. At least she'd thought it had been fantastic at the time. Unsettled by the thought, she bolted from the table and ran down the stairs toward her office, barely missing her unwanted guest as he was coming up. "Pardon me," he said, sidestepping out of her way. She took no notice of him and barreled on, slamming into her tiny office.

The windowless room was hardly bigger than a closet, bare cement walls and floor, without windows or adornment. When the three sisters first moved into the inn, a small cot had been crammed between the desk and the entry wall, giving Elissa a makeshift bedroom. Now she slept in the room that Helen had first used, then Lucy. The cot was thankfully long gone. In its place stood two gray metal filing cabinets.

Her secretary's chair was secondhand and worn, as was her metal desk and fax. But *by heaven* they were hers—just like her inn—and she loved every scratched, dented inch of each piece.

With fingers that would hardly function, she dialed her old professor and mentor at the University of Missouri law school. Though she prided herself on her independence, not leaning on anyone, she was no fool. She knew she needed professional guidance in this. And there was no one who knew the law like Dr. Grayson. When he came on the line, she worked to keep her voice even, placid, explaining what had happened.

By the time she sat down in her creaky chair, she was no longer trembling. Dr. Grayson had always been a calming influence and she felt a flood of relief, knowing that a man of such serene wisdom was on her side.

"Send me everything you have, Elissa. I'll see what I can find out."

She swallowed, her gratefulness making her teary. "Thanks, Dr. Grayson. I'd feel better with somebody who's up on things to go over this." Her voice breaking, she winced, then admitted as evenly as she could, "I'm afraid I can't be objective. This man is trying to take away my life."

There was silence for a moment, before Dr. Grayson spoke. "I hope we can find a loophole, dear."

There was another bothersome pause and Elissa's anxiety level soared. "What? What is it you're not telling me?"

"Nothing, dear. Nothing to worry about."

"Dr. Grayson," she insisted. "Tell me!"

He cleared his throat. "You shouldn't have left the law, Elissa. You have good instincts."

"What does that mean?"

"It means I do know something that might upset you. And I wish you weren't so intuitive to sense it."

"What is it?" She felt pain and realized she was digging into her knee with her nails.

"Well…" Her professor cleared his throat again. Not a good sign. "I've heard of Alex D'Amour. He's one hell-on-wheels litigator. You remember that Hildabrant Industries toxic waste suit out in California?''

She felt a surge of nausea. ''*He* won that?''

''Got a hundred million dollar settlement for the families in the affected area. I'm afraid he may be hard to beat.''

Elissa closed her eyes and sagged in her chair. ''Oh— Dr. Grayson. You have to find *something* to prove I'm the rightful owner. I've put every cent I've made back into this place. If I lose it, I'll have nothing.'' Her lips quivered and she pulled them between her teeth.

''Try not to worry. If there's a way to keep your inn, I'll find it.''

She nodded, but couldn't speak. Her voice was too quivery to trust.

''This is Sunday, so tomorrow, overnight-mail your documents to me. Okay?''

She cleared her throat, but her ''okay'' was fragile, almost undetectable. ''First thing.''

''And, Elissa…''

''Yes, Dr. Grayson?'' She toyed with the handle of a mug, half full of day-old coffee.

''Try to have a Merry Christmas.''

She inhaled unsteadily. ''I won't be merry until I know the inn is mine.''

''I'll do this as quickly as I can, but you know how things go. Especially around the holidays.''

''I know.'' She cringed, disconcerted that her turmoil was spilling over into her voice. She hardly ever cried, but she was right on the verge. ''Thanks…'' She whispered, swiping at a tear.

''Goodbye, dear.''

When he broke the connection, Elissa couldn't move.

She didn't know how long she sat there with the receiver clutched in her hand.

A knock at her office door made her jump, and she dropped the receiver. The clatter it made hitting the cement floor, then bouncing up into her metal desk, then dropping back to tap-dance across floor, was nerve-racking.

"Are you okay?" came a deep male voice.

She lurched to her feet, grabbing the receiver by the cord and drawing it up. "What do you want?" After a couple of fumbled tries, she managed to get the stubborn thing into the phone's cradle. "I'm busy."

"I need to use the fax."

"Don't you have some fancy laptop computer you could use?"

"Not on me."

She slumped to perch a hip on her desk, crossing her arms before her. "What if I told you you can't use mine?"

There was silence for a long minute, a silence that was far from reassuring. "What if I told you to get out of my inn, today?" he challenged.

She gasped. "I—I you *wouldn't!*"

"I need to use the fax."

He opened the door. Some small corner of her mind caught on the fact that he'd changed out of his dark three-piece suit and was now wearing soft beige trousers and a matching polo shirt. She was startled to note that he was more muscular than she might have expected of a man who spent his days drinking three-martini lunches and filing wordy briefs.

Formidable and grim, he stood there watching her with those breath-stealing eyes, his resolve electrifying the air around her. "Are you going to move, Miss Crosby?"

Never overly thrilled at being ordered around, she gritted her teeth and dug in her heels. "Have you heard of the phrase, 'When pigs fly,' Mr. D'Amour?"

He took a step toward her; the scratches along his jaw jumped as muscles flexed beneath the skin—a silent testament to his anger.

CHAPTER TWO

ELISSA had no idea what she thought she was doing, leaning against her desk, arms crossed belligerently. She was acting as though she intended to block Alex D'Amour from gaining access to her fax.

That was the most ludicrous idea she'd ever had, and her brain screamed, *Jump out of the way before he flattens you, idiot!* Nevertheless, her body resisted. Stubbornness was a flaw in Elissa's character—according to her sisters—but she had always thought of it more as, well, being right.

Elissa watched D'Amour lift his arms and she stiffened, visualizing herself being thrown through the office door. She clenched her teeth, warning in a low voice, "Go ahead—try to use my fax. If you dare." She lifted her chin. An instant too late it occurred to her that giving him such a conspicuous target wasn't very bright. *Okay, Mr. D'Amour,* she cried inwardly, *if you're looking for some knee-in-the-groin revenge, here's your chance!*

Two steps and Alex D'Amour was close enough to strike. A growl issued from his throat and he grasped her upper arm, tugging her away from the desk. Against her will, she cringed as he leaned around her. *He's not going to simply throw me out the door,* Elissa thought in panic, *he's going to throw me over his shoulder—and then out the door!*

His hand came down, rubbing hard across her backside—hardly what she'd expected. Instinctively she jumped sideways, only to be caught again as he returned to his rubbing. "What do you think you're doing?" she demanded, shocked and breathless.

"Hold still."

She wrenched at his grip, but he held her fast. The lethal glare she shot him missed its target, since his attention was focused on her back—her *hips* to be brutally precise. Furious, she shifted so that she could knee him the way she had that morning, but he deftly dodged the attempt, releasing her so suddenly she nearly fell.

"Only one free groin shot to a customer, Miss Crosby."

When she righted herself he had turned his back and was swabbing a handkerchief over her desktop, soaking up some dark liquid. Suddenly she realized what he was doing. "My coffee spilled?"

"It isn't mine." He refolded his handkerchief and sopped up the remainder of the liquid that was snaking toward the fax machine. Elissa inched up beside him, tentatively touching the seat of her wool skirt. She detected a faint dampness. Twisting around as far as she could, she squinted down at the herringbone pattern. "Did it stain?" She arched around until she'd turned in a full circle. But no matter how hard she tried, she couldn't see her rear end, much less a stain on her skirt.

His large hand on her shoulder halted her halfway through her second spin. "You remind me of a puppy chasing its tail," he said. "And no, it didn't stain." He held the soaked handkerchief toward her. "Where can I put this?"

She glowered at him as the harsh fluorescent light above his head accentuated his rugged good looks. Thick, black hair that tapered neatly to his collar gave off a soft luster, begging for fingers to stroke and caress. Tall and straight, he was a remote yet majestic figure, with the trace of silver at his temples and eyes that glowed like mercury. In other words, the man was sexy-as-hell. The instant the wayward thought surfaced in her mind, she squelched it, growing angrier. She had never acted like a fluttery female in her life, and she didn't intend to start now. Especially not because of *him!*

Mild amusement rode his gaze, hiking her agitation. Her lips parted with an urge to tell him exactly where he could put his handkerchief, but a rush of gratitude stopped her. His quick thinking had saved her favorite skirt. Before she could form an answer, his lips lifted in a sardonic smile. "I'll rephrase that. Where is your laundry room?"

Though she knew she should thank him, she stubbornly pursed her lips. Part of her wanted to tell him she was grateful, but most of her wanted him to take a flying leap off a cliff. She wasn't sure how it happened, but civility won out, and she nodded toward the office door. "The laundry room's across the hall." She extended a hand, surprising herself even more. "I'll take it."

He appeared as startled as she felt. "Thanks." He placed the dripping mess into her open palm. "Now, Miss Crosby, may I use your fax?"

She had pivoted toward the door. With his question, she halted, bitterness swelling inside her. He had some nerve asking her permission when they both knew what would happen if she refused. She turned back, her glare unblinking and reproachful. "I'm going to fight you on this, Mr. D'Amour. I'll prove my ownership." She paused, struggling to suck in a breath that didn't catch in her throat. "I may have to put up with you for a few days, but don't get the notion I believe you have any claim to my property. Once I get verification that this inn is mine, I'll call the police to have you tossed out on your ear. Do we understand each other?'' The last words were a rough whisper.

One dark brow curled upward. "Is that a yes?"

Her temper flared. She couldn't remember when she'd been this outraged. How dare he not be intimidated. She felt a spark of misgiving at that, but tried to reassure herself. *Mr. D'Amour is a lawyer, trained to disguise his emotions, to look supremely confident even when he's quaking with fear.* She'd been out of the profession a long time, and was rusty at the game. Unfortunately he was at the top of his.

For all her loathing of this man and his plans to take away her inn, she had to give him credit. He was good. He just stood there, watching her, making her doubt herself without saying a word.

She'd never met anyone who could affect her that way, and she had a sinking feeling he wasn't cloaking any fear with false calm. He was simply very sure of himself. That realization tore her confidence. *No!* She couldn't accept that. For if it were true, then she didn't own...

She fought back the thought, too horrible to allow full-blown into her mind. Digging deep within herself, she managed to straighten her face and square her shoulders, giving him back the same, self-assured air that he displayed so flawlessly. *Two could play at this game. Elissa Crosby did not cower or admit defeat!*

She managed a polite expression, a miracle, considering her internal turmoil. "Guests of my Inn may use the fax for free, Mr. D'Amour." She shifted to go, then glanced over her shoulder, her smile calculated. "I'll run *you* a tab."

Elissa's bravado was wearing thin. It had been a long day, especially considering how little sleep she'd had the night before, crouched in the D'Amour mansion closet. She hadn't realized the thought of going down to her bedroom would engender as much emotional chaos as spending the night in a frigid, cramped enclosure in fear for her life. But that's how she felt as she headed toward the basement stairs.

Since her staff had immediately recognized the D'Amour name, she'd told her housekeeper, her cook and her part-time assistant that Mr. D'Amour was going to be a neighbor. She had "been delighted" to offer him lodging while he was refurbishing his mansion. She had no intention of stirring up fears among her employees about the possibility of their losing their jobs. She wouldn't give that idea a moment of her time. It simply would *not* happen.

With her new, part-time employee manning the registration desk, Elissa trudged down the stairs. To her great discomfort, she would have to pass by Mr. Stealer-of-Dreams. When she opened the door to the basement, she noticed a light on, making it clear that he was still awake.

She decided she'd better knock before barging around the corner, though it grated on her nerves that she must make any concessions for this man. She rapped against the partially open door.

"Yes?" came a deep voice.

"I'd like to go to my room. Are you decent?"

"No, I'm buck naked."

Her cheeks warmed at the risqué vision that passed through her mind. The unexpected reaction irritated her, and she wasn't sure why. Stiff-backed she marched into the room. "Sarcasm is a poor excuse for humor, Mr. D'Amour." Though she'd vowed not to look at him, movement caught her attention and she turned, only to stumble to a halt as her unwelcome guest wrapped himself in a towel. "Oh..." she cried, feeling as though she'd been hit in the stomach.

"Thanks for that bulletin about sarcasm, Miss Crosby." He tucked the corner of his towel at his side to secure it. "But I rarely lie about being naked." He bent down to his open suitcase and plucked up what looked to be a shaving kit. Glancing narrowly at her, he headed for the bathroom that opened out into the basement parlor. His long legs ate up the distance, flexing calf and thigh muscles drawing her gaze. When he reached the door, he turned to lounge a shoulder against the jamb. "Did you say something?" An eyebrow rose in question.

She could do nothing but shake her head. Warring emotions squeezed her throat like a vise. She despised the man, but some basic womanly instinct sent a ripple of appreciation through her as she saw what a marvelous male specimen he was.

"Oh? Too bad." He appeared thoughtful. "I thought you might have apologized for barging in. My mistake."

Her face was flaming and had to be the same color as her hair. She attempted to speak, knowing she should atone, but no sound would come.

His lips curving in the vaguest smile, he slowly cocked a hip. Elissa caught the movement and stared, experiencing a lurch in her chest. With the lazy, calculated move, the ends of his towel separated nearly all the way up his thigh, leaving only his masculine essentials to the imagination. Unfortunately her imagination decided to go there with a vengeance. Pulling in a deep breath she belatedly forced her gaze to his face. She was appalled to see that his grin had grown shrewd. "Been a long time, huh?"

Her jaw almost hit the floor when she realized what he meant. Had she been obviously devouring him with her eyes? It was true that she hadn't dated anyone in a while. But running her inn was a twenty-four-hour-a-day job. Her lack of male companionship was her *choice*. Was he suggesting she was a poor, deprived old maid, lusting after him? *Him! Of all people in the world!* Realizing her mouth was open, she pressed her lips together and counted to ten. "I beg your pardon!" she finally demanded in a raspy whisper.

He straightened, deftly tossing the shaving kit from one hand to the other. "I accept your apology, Miss Crosby." His gaze taunting, he took a step back and closed the door between them.

She didn't know how long she stood there scowling, wishing looks could drill through doors and vaporize arrogant interlopers in their tracks. Her body fairly vibrated with fury. The man was impossible! How long could she bear to have him underfoot, acting so superior, so smug while insisting he owned *her* inn?

The click of a door opening made her start and she was mortified to be caught still rooted there like a potted geranium. When Mr. D'Amour came out of the bathroom this time, he was wearing a pair of gray shorts. He glanced her way, a sparkle coming to life in his eyes. "How nice—company," he said, without even a hitch in his step. It was as though he expected her to be there *waiting* for him. "What can I do for you now, Miss Crosby?"

He began to remove cushions from the sofa, preparing to open it up into a bed. Elissa watched him, noting the play of muscles along his arms and shoulders, the tautness of his belly as he bent over. Not an ounce of extra flesh bulged over the elastic waistband of his shorts. Blast him! As her mind began to wonder about how many sit-ups it might take to create a belly like his, he straightened. Holding a cushion, he gave her a rather amused, speculative look. She frowned. What had he asked?

Laying the cushion aside, he indicated the sofa. "I bet you stayed to help me open the bed." His eyes were challenging.

Her emotions jangling with embarrassment and indignation, she planted her hands on her hips. "Mr. D'Amour, the only thing I'd care to help you open is an artery." She jerked her head toward the bathroom. "There are clean sheets and blankets in the linen closet." In an icy monotone, she added, "Just so you're perfectly clear on this, I do *not* consider you a guest, I consider you an intruder."

His unwavering gaze disconcerted her. After a few ticks of the clock he nodded, then bent to tug open the bed. With a high-pitched creak, it unfolded revealing the thin mattress that covered the springs. When he straightened and looked at her again, he propped his fists on his hips in a gesture that was plainly mocking. "And just so you'll be perfectly clear, Miss Crosby, I do not consider myself a guest, either. I consider myself a property owner who is being very lenient with a squatter."

She gasped, horrified. *"Squatter!"* The suggestion was so outlandish it was laughable. She only wished she *could* laugh. "If I were you, Mr. D'Amour, I'd watch who I called a squatter. You're sleeping on *my* sofa, remember." She wheeled around toward her bedroom.

"Then maybe you should call me Alex."

She had taken hold of the doorknob when she started

to turn back, then decided against it. She might not be able to keep herself from hurdling the sofa bed and strangling him. How dare he bait her. She was no hypocrite. She didn't intend to call her worst enemy by anything as intimate as his first name, and he knew it. Especially not after *he* had suggested it. Too angry to trust her voice, she squeezed the doorknob until her knuckles whitened.

The silence between them grew heavy with tension. "Mr. D'Amour," she managed to say at last, "don't ever again wander around *my* inn—naked."

Elissa couldn't recall a time when her luck had been worse. As she opened her door the next morning, she found herself facing the obnoxious Alex D'Amour. His bed had been folded into a sofa again and he was dressed in a pair of jeans, work boots and a burgundy turtleneck sweater. He didn't look much like a high-powered California lawyer, today. When he noticed her, he spread his arms, palms up. "Okay?"

She frowned, puzzled. "What?"

He grinned. "I'm not naked."

Her cheeks blazing, she broke eye contact and barreled toward the stairs. "Mr. D'Amour will you please stop harassing me?"

"Harassing you?" He fell into step beside her. "I thought I was making a joke."

She reached the door at the bottom of the stairs before giving him a look that would ignite coal. "I don't want to joke with you, Mr. D'Amour," she said determinedly. "I don't want to speak to you. I don't want to *see* you. Does that make our relationship quite clear?"

His pleasant expression fading, he watched her for a strained moment before he took hold of the doorknob and turned it. "Quite clear, Miss Crosby." Stepping back he allowed her to precede him. "I'm going to need a table. My contractor is coming by this morning with the remodeling plans."

Much to Elissa's dismay, he kept up with her on the stairs. Her shoulder brushed his arm several times and his scent was hard to miss in the confined stairway—something like tobacco with a trace of cedar. She inhaled deciding the scent was pleasantly manly. What a shame it was wasted on Alex D'Amour.

"Miss Crosby?" Hearing him speak pulled her back. She glanced his way as they reached the top of the stairs. "A table?" he repeated.

She was startled that she'd let her mind drift away. With a disgruntled exhale, she faced him. "In the parlor there's a bridge table in the corner that isn't used often."

He nodded. "I'm sure I can find it. Don't trouble yourself."

"Don't worry."

They were in the short hallway where the basement staircase faced the back door. To their left was the kitchen, to the right was the staircase hall and dining room.

"Something smells good," he said.

Ignoring him, Elissa turned into the kitchen where every burner on the stove held a steamy pot or pan. Somehow, Bella managed to feed twelve to fifteen guests breakfast every day and still keep the kitchen spotless. Elissa glanced around at the familiar Monday morning fare: blueberry waffles, sausages, scrambled eggs, choices of juices, coffee or tea. It smelled like heaven in the homey kitchen. Elissa greeted the plump cook with as carefree a wave as she could manage. "How's it coming, Bella? Full house?"

Bella chortled, swiping her forehead with the hem of her starched apron. "Yes, ma'am. You know how it is here at Christmas. So much to do, everybody wanting to get up and out and about."

Elissa knew all too well. In Branson the Christmas season was their busiest, next to summer. By many it was considered the best time to visit, with their Ozark Mountain Christmas and spectacular Festival of Lights. And with two hundred factory outlet stores, the Ozark's "Little Las Vegas" was a Mecca for Christmas shoppers. Elissa had grown to love the holidays in Branson, with its quaint, country appeal. The idea of having to leave tore at her.

Bella said something, and Elissa tried to refocus on business. "Yes?"

"I said half the guests were waiting for me at seven. So most everybody's already eaten."

Elissa glanced at her watch. "Really? It's only seven-thirty now."

Bella's lilting chortle filled the warm kitchen. "I guess we don't have any late-sleepers this week."

Elissa managed a smile. "Then, you'll get a nice long break this morning."

Bella nodded. "I plan to put my feet up, have some coffee and daydream."

"Have any of the guests signed up to be here for dinner tonight or are they all staying in town?"

"Town," Bella said with a smile. "Except for that charming Mr. D'Amour. He'll be here." Shuffling to the stove, she stirred a fresh batch of eggs. "Nice intimate dinner, just you two. A pleasant way to get to know your neighbor, don't you think?" Shifting back, her expression grew expectant. "Fine looking man, that Mr.

D'Amour. And so rich. You two make a handsome couple, I'd say.''

Elissa blanched, peering over her shoulder to see if the ''fine looking'' man in question was standing there. For once luck was with her. Apparently he'd gone to join the others in the dining room. Breathing a sigh, she glanced at her cook, trying not to show her aversion to the idea of eating alone with the man. ''Oh—Mr. D'Amour is just a—a—new neighbor, Bella. That's all there is to it.''

The cook didn't appear convinced, but glanced away as the waffle iron light indicated another batch was done. ''Of course, Miss Elissa, now you go on and have yourself some breakfast.'' She waved a spatula toward the dining room. ''There's only that cute Thoron couple and the Parracks left. And—'' Bella shambled over to get the waffle serving plate off the kitchen table, glancing at Elissa ''—and your new *neighbor*.'' She smiled shrewdly, and Elissa didn't like the look of it. Clearly the fact that Mr. D'Amour was sleeping in the basement had started the gossip going among the help. Why hadn't she thought of that? Did they think she was having a quickie affair with a man she'd just met? Well, that couldn't be helped. She supposed it was better than having them panicking about losing their jobs right before Christmas.

She contrived a smile and pivoted toward the pantry, the shortcut into the dining room. The first sound that assailed her was the rich laughter of her unwelcome lodger. She stepped through the door, distressed to see the young couple, Mr. and Mrs. Thoron leaving. The Parracks were already gone. Mr. D'Amour stood to shake Mr. Thoron's hand and nod toward his petite wife. Bella's gaunt, silent kitchen helper, Ramona, was clearing away dishes, her eyes downcast, as she pretended not to exist.

When Alex D'Amour started to seat himself, he saw Elissa lingering in the pantry entrance, and remained standing. "Are you joining me, Miss Crosby?"

She felt caught. Timid Ramona was approaching the pantry entrance burdened with dirty dishes, clearly unsettled that the doorway was blocked. Sidestepping into the dining room, Elissa gave the poor, shy dear an escape route.

As uncomfortable as she could ever remember being, Elissa fought for poise. "I was going to get a cup of coffee," she lied, heading for the sideboard where the coffee urn sat. Grabbing a mug, she held it beneath the spigot trying to ignore the feel of his gaze on her back.

"The food's delicious," he said.

"Of course it is." With an irritated swipe she shut off the valve and shifted to scowl at him. "I'm offended that you're continually surprised by the quality of my inn, Mr. D'Amour."

"Alex," he said, returning his attention to his plate and taking up his fork. "Don't let your pride make you go hungry, Elissa. Sit down. Eat."

Her fingers tightened on her mug. "Don't call me Elissa," she spat in a whisper. "We are *not* friends."

He peered her way. "Can't you understand that I'm not stealing this place from you. It's mine. If you'd care to show me receipts I'll reimburse you for any improvements you've made." He shifted in his chair, leaning a forearm on the tablecloth to better face her. "I don't want to be unfair."

Receipts? Improvements? What about the inn itself? She and her sisters had pooled every penny they had in order to buy it. Besides, running this place was her dream, her life. And he talked about unfair? It seemed that the loss of a person's life savings and dreams were insignificant details to this tough-as-nails litigator, who obviously had a calculator for a heart. Hysterical laugher gurgled in her throat. "Well, Mr. D'Amour, aren't you a prince." Slamming the mug on the table she eyed him with hostility. "If you'll excuse me, I have business in town."

Though Elissa found herself tensing up every time she went out to the mailbox, she was relieved that there had been no more threatening letters. Thank heaven. The first one that frightened her so, had undoubtedly been a random act by someone with too much time on his hands and very little social conscience. Hadn't the police suggested just that? And since there weren't any discernible fingerprints on the letter, their investigation had gone nowhere, anyway.

With great relief, she put her silly fears from her mind, determining to move on. She had enough troubles with Alex D'Amour and his very real threat to take away her property.

The inn remained filled to capacity all week, and Elissa was too busy to dwell on the Alex D'Amour problem. She was grateful for small favors.

Though he was gone most of the day with his contractors, he invariably returned in time for dinner. A couple of evenings that week, new arrivals checked in just in time for the evening meal, but even with extra people present, Elissa couldn't choke down her food while those cold eyes hounded her every move. After the third evening under his scrutiny, she'd made an excuse to Bella that she had a lot of paper work to do, and ate the rest of her evening meals at her desk.

Tonight, she couldn't even force down her food in the privacy of her office. She kept checking her watch. Any minute her sisters and their families would arrive. What was she going to do about Mr. D'Amour? What was she going to tell her sisters? She couldn't ruin their Christmas with the news that she might lose the inn as well as their investment in it.

And worse. Her old law professor, Dr. Grayson, had no good news about her ownership. No news, really. The holidays were a terrible time to try to get anything done. It seemed that anyone in government offices who had any authority was on vacation. She was so frustrated she wanted to scream.

She toyed with her coffee cup, closing her eyes in a silent prayer that this would not be the last Christmas she would spend here. And, if the worst happened and it was, that this holiday not be spoiled for her sisters by the heartless heir to the D'Amour property.

A knock at the office door jarred her, and her eyes snapped open. "Who is it?"

"Alex. I need to use your fax."

She bowed her head, fighting off a bout of anxious queasiness. "Come in," she called. "We need to talk."

The door squeaked opened, and Elissa pushed up from her chair, straightening her navy wool skirt more out of uneasiness than need.

"This is unusual," he said as she twisted to face him. "No hurling insults? No barring of the door? No threats of beheading?" He stopped behind her chair, brows lifting in question. "I gather you've poisoned my stew and you want to watch me die."

She crossed her arms before her and sat back against her desk. "My favorite fantasy—but no."

He cocked his head, looking cautious. "I know you

haven't heard good news from your lawyer friend, because there won't be any.''

She gritted her teeth, biting back a sharp denial. She didn't have the luxury of time to fight with him. ''Look,'' she said through a resigned sigh. ''I have to ask you a favor.''

His gaze narrowed, and she could see high skepticism in his expression. ''I refuse to jump off the roof.''

Eyeing heaven, she clutched her hands together. ''Be serious.'' She checked her watch again, then reclasped her hands. ''There's not much time.''

The crease in his brow deepened. ''For what?''

''My...'' She swallowed. ''My family is coming for Christmas. I don't want them upset by this—this misunderstanding about the inn.''

''Miss Crosby, you must face the—''

''*So!*'' she interrupted, ''I want you to go along with my plan to tell them we're old friends from law school.''

''Law school?'' He looked skeptical. ''What are you, around thirty, thirty-two, tops? I'm thirty-eight, Miss Crosby. I graduated from Harvard Law, and I was in practice before you—''

''Okay, okay!'' She shook her head. ''Say we met at some law conference or something.''

''And what?''

Unsettled by his cross examination, she broke eye contact, absently scanning the gray cement walls. ''I don't know. We became friends, I suppose. What else?''

''No. We had an affair.''

She jerked to stare at him. *''What?''*

He shrugged, his eyes glittering eerily. ''Why else would I be here?''

''Lots of men have platonic female friends.''

''I don't.'' His grin was revealing. The woman in her

knew—without a doubt—that no female who had ever befriended Alex D'Amour had *any* desire to keep the relationship platonic. "This could be fun," he went on. "Of course, if we use that lie, I'd have to sleep with you."

She stared, stunned, then saw the sparkle in his eyes and realized he was baiting her. "That's very funny, Mr. D'Amour. Does that line work for you?"

"Apparently not." He grinned crookedly, clearly far from crushed by her rejection. "It's worth thinking about, though."

"Let me do the thinking. It's less dangerous."

"If you must." He placed his hands on the back of her office chair. "But, while you're thinking, Miss Crosby, think K-I-S-S."

She scowled at him. Couldn't he get off sex? Did he think he was so irresistible that she would be willing to stoop to anything to get his help? "Mr. D'Amour, do you do *all* your thinking with your—"

"Keep it simple, stupid," he interjected. "Didn't you learn that in law school? K-I-S-S."

As the acronym soaked in, her cheeks heated. Just who was the one who couldn't get her mind off sex? "Oh…"

"I find that the simplest story is usually the best. If you must lie to your family, tell them I own the D'Amour mansion, that I'm staying here while it's re-modeled and that we've become friends."

After a moment, she nodded, acknowledging that the idea had merit. "And—and since you didn't have a res-ervation," she improvised, "I had to put you down here in the basement."

His expression had grown serious. A tensing along his

jaw drew her attention. "What's wrong now? It was your idea."

He leaned forward, over the chair back. Elissa had the urge to clamber onto her desk to put distance between them, but she resisted. "Are you sure you want to lie? Wouldn't you rather have your family join you in staring daggers at me?"

"Of course I would," she admitted, then shook her head. "But I want their holiday here to be happy. Besides, once I've proven my ownership, they'll never have to know there was a problem." Making reluctant eye contact, she tried to seem confident, but the act was tainted when she adjusted her suit jacket and toyed with the buttons.

He clenched his jaw. "I may joke about it, Miss Crosby, but frankly, I don't like lying."

"I don't care what you like." She bit her tongue. This was no time to make him mad. Shaking herself for her outburst she eased her features and her voice. "If you have an ounce of humanity in you, you'll do this for my family's sake."

He eyed her with cynicism. "I don't give a damn about families."

"Miss Elissa!" came Bella's shout from the top of the stairs. "Your sisters are here."

Witnessing Alex D'Amour's unyielding expression, Elissa's heart fell into a deep, dark well.

CHAPTER THREE

ALEX D'AMOUR'S expression was uncompromising, and panic rose inside Elissa. What could she offer this ruthless man to make him help her? In a last-ditch attempt, she pleaded, "I'm begging you, Mr. D'Amour." Her voice cracked, and she hated the sound of her weakness. Hated to have to ask anything of him.

She'd always been the strong one, the big sister Helen and Lucy depended on—ever since Mother had died. She'd only been nine, but her grief-stricken father had been no comfort to the three young girls. Even after Elissa had gone to law school she'd been there for her family, calling home every night to make herself available to listen to their problems or fears. Daddy had come to depend on her, too, when the illness that finally took his life incapacitated him. Helen and Lucy continued to count on her. She'd been mothering her sisters almost all their lives, and she didn't intend to fail them now.

She would not allow Alex's claim on her property to cast a pall over the holidays. She saw her sisters so rarely since they'd married, she refused to inflict pain on them during their short visit. But in order to protect them, she needed Alex D'Amour's help.

Swallowing to steady her voice, she asked, just above a whisper, "If you won't do it for my family, what—what *would* you do it for?"

A muscle flexed in his jaw, emphasizing the place where she had wounded him nearly a week ago. Shuttered eyes scanned her face, making her feel like a

39

flea about to be swatted. As time stretched into an agonizing eternity, her emotions became as taut as violin strings. Finally he muttered, "I'll do it for you."

She was confused, not sure she'd heard right. "For—*me?*" Visions of demanded sexual favors flashed through her mind. She bit out her reply, "No matter how badly I need your help, I won't sleep with you."

His low chuckle was humorless. "Don't panic, Miss Crosby, I don't force women into my bed." He turned away, presenting her with his grim profile. "I just figure I can do that much for you."

She could hardly believe what she was hearing. He'd agreed, and there were no strings. Clearly he was less than delighted about it, but he was going to keep the secret. That's what mattered.

Overwhelmed with gratitude, she stumbled around the chair and threw her arms around his neck, hugging him. "Oh, thank you! Thank you, Mr. D'Amour." She could feel his body go taut against hers in his surprise, and that reminded her exactly who he was and why he was there. *What did she think she was doing?* She backed away, mortified.

She noticed his hands had stilled in a half-raised position, almost a defensive gesture. She came close to smiling about that. Could she blame him for anticipating an attack? After all, the only other times she'd made contact with his body she'd clawed him, kneed him, then *tried* to knee him, again.

Avoiding his gaze she focused on his cleft chin, striving to appear all business. "Uh, you can call me Elissa and I'll call you Alex. Okay?"

He smiled, but there was precious little humor there. "Why didn't I think of that."

"Miss Elissa?" Bella called again.

Her heart constricted. "Oh dear…" Was she going to be able to carry off this farce? Could she keep her worries from her family? "Oh—dear…"

A hand, big and warm, encircled her elbow. Until that second, she hadn't realized how cold she was. "Let's go, Elissa dear." He tugged her into movement. "How's this?" Light-headed with trepidation, she glanced at his face. He grinned down at her in a way that reeked of affection. *He was really good.* "Now you try," he coaxed.

She inhaled, attempting to arrange her face in a smile.

He chuckled as she battled to fake a pleasant demeanor. "This is your lie, Miss Crosby. If you want to look believable, unclench your teeth."

She tried again.

"Better." He aimed her toward the steps. "Should I put my arm around you?"

"No!" She drew away. "We don't have to be that friendly. Maybe just, er, acquaintances is fine. The point is, I don't want you to mention the—you know." She could feel her nerve draining away. It had never occurred to her that her little white lie might include physical contact.

He took her arm again when he saw that she was hesitating. "Okay, Miss Acquaintance. Just so we're *acquainted* enough that we don't claw each other in the face or knee each other in our private parts. Deal?"

She slanted him a look, her lips twitching in what was trying to be a smile. Darn the man; his easygoing charm was getting to her. Apparently her gratefulness was making her feeble-witted. "I make no promises."

Laughter rumbled in his throat. "I love a woman of mystery."

The mellow timbre of his mirth rankled her, not so

much because she didn't like the sound of it, but because she did.

Much of Elissa's anxiety melted away when she entered the noisy commotion going on in the reception hall. Her sisters, Lucy and Helen, and their husbands, Jack and Damien, laughed and chatted and carried in luggage. Since their flights had arrived within the same hour, they'd decided to rent a car and drive down from Springfield together.

When Elissa spied her nieces, Gilly and Glory, scampering among a forest of suitcases and adult legs, she managed a real smile. Hurrying into the fray, she hunkered down to toddler level. "Where are my girls?" She stretched out welcoming arms. "How about a kiss for Aunt Elissa?"

Giggly squeals answered her. Seconds later she was plowed into by twin, chubby projectiles, who had their daddy's dark hair and their mommy's bright, gray eyes. Shy little Elissa Gillian, her namesake, planted a cool, sloppy kiss on her cheek.

Elissa hugged them close, her heart turning over with a mixture of joy and sadness. Where would they all be a year from today? Shaking off the thought, she stood, hoisting the twins in her arms. She would do no negative thinking. "Okay, you all can go now," she kidded. "I have my Christmas presents."

"Okay, Red," Damien teased, his arm around Helen's waist. "If you want the little darlings, they're yours. But I warn you, they're almost into their terrible two's."

Helen jabbed him with an elbow. "Hush. She'll take you up on it."

He laughed, releasing his wife to kiss his encumbered sister-in-law. "How've you been?" Damien's gaze searched her face as though he detected something was wrong. Even half-blind and sporting an eyepatch, he was much too perceptive. "I'm about to keel over," she lied with a forced laugh. "What have you been feeding these young ladies, rocks?" Handing the giggling, squirming toddlers to their daddy, she embraced Helen, kissing her cheek. "You look fabulous," she whispered. "Damien must be doing his job."

Helen laughed. "Oh, yes." She kissed her sister back. "Yes indeed."

"Hey," came another familiar male voice. "Where's my kiss?"

Elissa released her baby sister and grinned at her other brother-in-law, Jack Gallagher. With mock consternation, she shook her head at him. "You're getting handsomer; you aren't supposed to do that. You're supposed to go fat and lose all that sexy brown hair."

He winked at her, pulling her into his embrace. "And you're supposed to get hippy and crotchety."

"Why, Jack," she said with affront. "I pride myself on my crotchetiness, and I'm working on hippy."

Jack laughed as they hugged. Lucy came up to take her sister's hands. "It's good to be back. The place is beautiful with all the decorations. I love the lights and greenery around the windows. It looked so festive as we drove up. I can't imagine anywhere else on earth where I'd rather spend Christmas."

Lucy's heartfelt statement stabbed Elissa, but she hid the pain. When her sister's soft blue eyes lifted over Elissa's shoulder, her smile grew curious. "Who's this?" Elissa's stomach churned. She knew exactly who Lucy meant.

Hesitantly she shifted to peer at Alex as he watched the hustle and bustle, his expression oddly troubled. She was surprised. She'd expected to see that really-good-lie-of-a-grin on his face. Before she had time to react, Damien walked up to the stranger, extending a hand around the fidgety bundle he was holding in the crook of that arm. "I'm Damien Lord, and the pretty lady in the maroon tunic and leggings is Helen, my wife. These wiggly-worms are our girls, Gillian and Gloriana.

Helen extended a hand, which Alex took. Then by some sort of identical-twin brain wave, two pudgy baby hands flew out, flapping in a childish burlesque of their parents actions. Though Alex had released Helen's fingers, Elissa noted that he looked puzzled about the girls, not seeming to know what to do. Clearly he didn't have any experience with females under the age of consent. "I'm Alex D'Amour." He gave Damien an inquiring look. "Aren't you the author and political columnist?"

"Yes," Damien said with a grin. "And aren't you the lawyer who won that big toxic waste case in California not long ago?"

Now it was Alex's turn to smile. "Ex-lawyer. I've decided to become a gentleman landowner. Between the Santa Anna fires, earthquakes and working eighty hours a week, I knew some changes had to be made in my life."

"D'Amour?" Helen repeated with a gasp. "The same D'Amour who owns the estate?"

"The same."

Touching her husband's arm, she said, "Then you must have met Damien before. He rented it from you a few years back."

"No, honey," Damien said. "A friend of mine knew a lawyer in New York who was overseeing the property for the heirs. I rented it through the lawyer."

"My parents live in Europe, "Alex said. "Since there

was no will, my father inherited the property. He could never bring himself to sell it, but didn't have much use for a drafty old place in the boonies. Then last summer a will was found in a piece of furniture that belonged to my grandparents' lawyer, who died around the same time they did, when I was five. Until the desk was sold at auction a few months ago, no one knew a will existed.''

''And that will left the property to you?'' Helen asked with a delighted smile.

Alex grinned back, his dimples appallingly sexy. ''Right. I was only notified last spring that I'd inherited. That was the catalyst for me to make the move.''

Elissa gathered her composure and wove her way through bodies and baggage to stand beside him, desperately uncomfortable, but determined. She smiled with difficulty, knowing it was time to call this—this—*trespasser* by his first name. ''Isn't it nice that Alex is going to restore the mansion?'' she said, rushing on, ''He's staying here during the remodeling—since my inn's so convenient.'' She faced Alex, working to make her smile look real. ''Isn't that right?''

He grinned down at her, and though she knew his expression was as false as hers, it was breathtaking, with those lush-lashed silver eyes and deep, slashing dimples. ''Exactly, Elissa.'' His gaze was so affectionate she wanted to kick him. He was doing it on purpose, the conniving bum! Wasn't he causing her enough trouble without this?

''Well, well…'' Lucy came forward hand in hand with Jack. She looked speculatively at her elder sister. ''You're both ex-lawyers and you're neighbors, too. How nice.'' She took his hand. ''It's so good to meet you, Alex. Your mansion has played a strong part in our lives. Of course Elissa has told you about that." She smiled up at him.

His grin broadened, which was no surprise to Elissa. Lucy, beautiful and blond, had turned more than one man to mush with that smile. "Really?" He lifted a brow. "No, Elissa hasn't said a thing."

"The D'Amour myth? You do know about the myth," Lucy prodded.

With Alex's puzzled expression, Elissa grew nervous. The last thing she needed was for her sisters to discover she'd slept inside the mansion on her birthday. Under a full moon, yet!

She certainly had no intention of letting them find out that Alex had been the first man she'd seen that morning. Since both Helen and Lucy believed in the silly story, that bit of news would only complicate an already lousy problem.

"No, I don't believe I've heard of any myth."

"Uh, Alex, have you met Jack Gallagher?" Elissa interjected abruptly. "He owns a few restaurants here and there." She hoped her tone was lighthearted, because she sure didn't feel that way. "The newest one is right here in Branson."

Alex's gaze shifted to Jack, who was hovering protectively beside his wife. "No kidding?" He withdrew his hand from Lucy's and took Jack's in a firm grip. "I've eaten at the Gallagher's Bistro in L.A. Great steaks. Is that yours?"

"Guilty, counselor." Jack grinned. "One of these nights we'll all have to go into town and eat at the Gallagher's here."

Elissa rolled her eyes. This was going way too well. They weren't supposed to welcome him into the clan, just tolerate him.

"You have quite a family, Elissa," Alex said, drawing her gaze. "You didn't tell me your brothers-in-law were famous." His perusal roamed appreciatively from Lucy to Helen, then back to Jack. "If Elissa had told me her sisters were as beautiful as she was, I wouldn't have believed it."

Elissa stared at Alex, absolutely flummoxed by the out-of-the-blue compliment. What a shame he'd given up the law. He could dish out the bull as smoothly as any attorney she'd ever seen.

She caught both Lucy and Helen looking at her with designing glints in their eyes, and swallowed with difficulty. Darn that Alex D'Amour. He was overdoing it. She'd have to straighten out her sisters later. "Well, we'd better get you all settled in." Restless and needing to escape Alex D'Amour's close scrutiny, she grabbed the first bag she saw. "Okay, Damien, you and Jack are in the room Damien used when he stayed here. Lucy, you and Helen can have the front corner room with the oriel."

Damien chuckled. "I don't think so." Allowing the squirmy girls to get down and scamper around, he took his sister-in-law's hand. "Not that I don't like Jack, but I'm old-fashioned. I figure I ought to get to share a room with the mother of my children."

Elissa flushed. "Sorry. I don't know where my mind is."

Lucy glanced from her older sister to the tall, dark man standing beside her. "I wonder?"

Elissa ignored the innuendo and headed for the stairs. "Everybody grab something."

Lucy squealed and giggled. "Jack! Elissa meant a *suitcase*." She playfully slapped his hand away from her bottom.

Elissa turned back. "Do I have to hose you two down? You've been married for almost two years. You should be sick to death of each other by now."

Jack's chuckle was wicked, and Elissa could only grin at him. "Okay, we'll hurry." In feigned dismay, she shook her head at the couple.

As she turned toward the staircase, she saw Alex pick up two big valises. Her surprise made her hesitate. She watched him for another second to make sure she was seeing right. When she realized he was truly helping, she had a fleeting urge to say thank-you, but her simmering bitterness overrode her gratitude. A spiteful voice in her head hissed, *"Good! Let's put him to work!"*

Elissa stretched and yawned. She was so emotionally drained she could hardly think. But there was one thing she had to take care of before she fell into her bed. She stood at the bathroom sink, towel-drying her hair. Staring at her pinched face in the mirror, she watched her green eyes flash with animosity. Alex D'Amour was going to get an earful as soon as His Majesty decided to come downstairs.

The last time she'd seen him, he was sitting at the kitchen table, drinking coffee and visiting with Damien and Helen as the twins played "uh-oh"—tossing bits of their dinner into the air, squealing a delighted *"uh-oh"* as food plummeted to the scrubbed floor. Elissa's laughter hadn't aided in Damien's and Helen's attempt to instill correct meal etiquette into their daughters, so she'd excused herself.

She prayed the conversation continued in the direction of Damien's latest novel. She didn't want the myth to come up at all.

As she combed through her damp curls, she heard

Alex enter the basement. Since she'd left the bathroom door open to make sure she caught him the instant he came downstairs, she spun to confront him. Tugging the lapels of her terry robe together, she stormed into the basement parlor.

He was closing the door to the stairway when she spotted him. Purposely she slammed the bathroom door and his head jerked up to see her glowering at him. As he scanned her, his expression changed from surprise to mischievous. Her knee-length robe was fuzzy aqua terry-cloth. Goofy slippers swallowed her feet. He leaned against the wall, visibly amused. "I pictured you more as a Garfield slippers kind of woman."

She gritted her teeth, having forgotten she was wearing the gift Helen had sent her for her birthday, saying the slippers were "from the twins, so they could all look alike this Christmas." Trying to ignore his taunt, she crammed her hands into her pockets. "What is it with you?" she demanded. "I wanted you to act like an acquaintance, not my lover. What was with all the hot-to-trot eye contact and rip-off-my-shirt-baby grinning?"

He laced his fingers at his waist, templing his thumbs over his belt buckle. Wearing jeans, work boots and a beige Henley shirt, he looked more like a woodsman than a big-city lawyer. "Was I doing all that?" he asked, his tone teasing.

She harrumphed. "I don't think you're funny. Cut the wattage, buster, or you'll find yourself doubled over groaning in pain, again."

He winced playfully. "Yes, ma'am."

She looked pointedly at him, unconvinced by his easy capitulation. "I *mean* it."

Pushing himself away from the wall, he ambled toward the couch and began removing cushions. "I read you loud and clear, Miss Crosby.'' He glanced her way. ''But if you don't get me a room of my own soon, it won't matter what I do. They'll draw their own conclusions.'' She felt the weight of his statement and dodged his intent gaze. He was right, of course. But there was nothing she could do about that.

''I'm all booked to New Year's Eve.'' Frustration edged her words. When he'd first come to the inn with his threats and legal papers, she'd relegated him to the fold-out couch, wanting him to be as miserable as possible. At the time, she'd been so angry this complication hadn't really bothered her. ''If there's a cancellation—and I *pray* there is—'' she vowed, ''you're out of here. Honestly, I'd rather have a rattlesnake sharing my quarters.''

He stared at her for another millisecond, just long enough for a lightning flash in his glance to inform her that her insult had hit its mark. Turning away, he yanked the Hide-A-Bed out with a screech of metal on metal. ''You're quite welcome, Miss Crosby,'' he muttered. ''Think nothing of it.''

Sunday morning, all the guests were fed and gone before Elissa's sisters and their families came downstairs. She was happy to have only her relations sitting around the breakfast table. Except for the pleasant addition of babies and husbands, this morning's gathering reminded Elissa of when the three of them had first bought the inn almost four years ago.

The only fly in the ointment was Alex D'Amour, whose contractors didn't work on Sundays. What a shame. Another blot on her day was the way her sisters had maneuvered to get her seated at the table beside Alex.

She exhaled a slow, defeated sigh. She'd tried to tell both Lucy and Helen that she and Alex were merely acquaintances, nothing more, but that information had been about as effective on her beaming sisters as trying to teach a newborn baby how to cook. They imagined a romance in the making and not even kicking and screaming and beating her breast was going to change their minds. She decided the best idea was to be coolly friendly to Alex, while remembering *not* to give away her distaste for the man. She only hoped her conversation with him last night had made an impression.

Damien and Helen sat on one side of the big table with the twins on high chairs between them. Between bites of their own breakfast, each parent was keeping an eye on a twin's plate, making sure it didn't end up stuck to a wall.

Elissa and Alex, Lucy and Jack sat across from them. Elissa noticed Helen had stopped eating and was watching Lucy closely. Before Elissa had time to ask what had captured her attention, Helen said, "Lucy, you're picking at your oatmeal. Are you okay?"

Elissa peered around Alex. "Luce? Would you rather have something else?" She shook her head, smiling wanly. "Oatmeal. Yuck. It's fine for the toothless babies, but not for adult types with full-grown taste buds."

The rest of them were eating buttermilk pancakes with maple syrup, a fruit cup and Bella's famous chicken hash. Why anyone would prefer oatmeal was beyond Elissa.

Lucy smiled weakly, her cheeks going pink from the attention. She laid her spoon into the half-full bowl of congealing muck. "I guess I'm just not very—" She bit off her words, pressing her fingers to her lips. The cast of her skin had gone a little green. "Jack..." She pressed her palms on the table, attempting to stand.

Her husband took her elbow. "I'll come with you, darling." A few seconds later the couple had made a hasty exit up the stairs.

Elissa was concerned. "I hope she's not sick. What an awful way to spend Christmas."

Helen frowned, turning to meet Damien's puzzled gaze. As Elissa watched, they both slowly began to smile, as though some great revelation had come to them. An instant later, it dawned on Elissa what was going on. "Lucy's going to have a baby," she breathed, tears of happiness gathering in her eyes. "Oh, that's wonderful." She had no idea she'd clamped a hand on Alex's upper arm and squeezed his solid biceps until the direction of Helen's gaze and the gleam in her eyes told her so. Abruptly she dropped her hand. "Excuse me," she muttered, grabbing her fork and shoveling up a pile of chicken hash.

"No problem, Elissa," he murmured. "It's hardly the first time we've touched."

She had taken a big bite, and his veiled innuendo sent her into a coughing spasm. She eyed him narrowly as she got herself under control but decided it would be better not to respond. The less said the better.

"Do you think I should go up and help Lucy?" Helen asked Damien as she deftly caught a half-chewed piece of banana that Glory had just "uh-ohed" into space.

When she put the squishy mess back on her daughter's plate, Damien said, "I think Jack wants to handle it, sweetheart." He captured a torn piece of toast in midair and gathered it back in Gilly's hand. "Okay, young lady. One more 'uh-oh' and no peaches."

Elissa watched Gilly make a face as she turned the

toast into pulp against her lips. Hardly able to contain a laugh, she glanced at Glory who was nearly through finger-feeding herself her serving of sliced canned peaches. With a grin she couldn't contain, she thought Damien and Helen were the cutest parents she'd ever seen—with great coordination, too, considering they could snag food as well as any major league baseball player ever snagged a hot, bouncing grounder.

Helen looked at Elissa. "Alex tells us you met him on the D'Amour property last week." She inclined her head. "What day?"

Elissa knew where this was going and she was determined to put a stop to it.

"I'll never forget it," Alex interjected, "It was—" He stopped in midsentence with his mouth opened. Instead of words, he emitted a guttural grunt, and his eyes went wide.

Helen and Damien stared at him, looking as though they were afraid he was having a heart attack. Elissa knew what was wrong, and it wasn't a medical emergency. She'd kicked him hard in the leg. "Are you okay?" she asked sweetly.

Alex faced her, his flashing gaze demanding why in the hell she kept trying to cripple him. With thinned lips he nodded. "Yeah. I'm great. Thanks for asking."

She smiled. "Well, if you're sure."

"Alex?" Helen said. "You looked like you had a pain. Don't be brave. What if it's serious?"

With his jaw working he shifted toward Helen. "It's not. I just forgot what I was going to say. I hate it when I do that."

Elissa had a hard time suppressing a grin at his weak excuse. She supposed he didn't get kicked under a table often enough to be very good at it.

"You must," Helen murmured, her expression confused.

Surprising everyone, Alex pushed up from the table and grabbed Elissa's wrist. "I'd like a word with you in private."

She wanted to say no, but she could feel hard resolve in his grasp. Having no option but to drop her fork, she smiled stiffly. "Why, certainly—Alex." Facing her sister and brother-in-law, she made an effort to appear at ease, though she had a sick feeling he planned to kick her back once they were alone. "We'll just be a minute."

Alex towed her from the room. "Maybe longer."

After he whisked her down the basement steps, he shut the door and turned on her. "What the hell was that kick for?" His grip held her captive. "Technically, that's battery, Miss Crosby. I could have you arrested."

"*Technically,* so is what you're doing." She yanked on his hold. "You're hurting me."

"Bull."

When she yanked again, he released her so swiftly she stumbled. When she steadied herself, she faced him with bravado. "And just what was that 'It's hardly the first time we've touched' remark? You made it sound like we're having an affair. I told you to back off the innuendos."

"I'm sorry. It just came out."

She eyed him with distrust, trying to decide if he was sincere. He wasn't smiling, and he seemed earnest. Her ire sputtered, dying down in the face of his apparently genuine apology. "Okay, I'm sorry I kicked you," she admitted. "It's only that I don't care to talk about when or where we met."

"Why the hell not?" he demanded. "They know I

own the D'Amour place. When and where we met doesn't compromise our deal.''

''It does to me.''

He ran a hand through his hair, clearly annoyed. ''I don't get it. Maybe you'd better tell me all the rules so I don't have to spend so much time limping or doubled-over gasping for breath.''

''That's all, Mr. D'Amour. Just don't mention the real reason you're staying here or that we met on your grounds last Sunday morning.'' She held out a hand. ''Deal?''

He eyed her outstretched fingers. Wariness riding his features, he leaned against the basement door and crossed his arms over his chest. ''There's more to this than you're telling me. Come clean or there's no deal.''

His insight bothered her. ''It's not important. It's nothing.''

He snorted. ''That *nothing* is going to turn into a nice size bruise on my shin. So it's not nothing to me. Spill it or I'll tell them the truth.''

''But you promised!''

He shrugged. ''You assaulted me, Miss Crosby. Do I hear why you did it, or do I tell your family you bought this property in a fraudulent deal, and that you're losing it after the new year.''

''*It's not true!*'' Fingers of dread crawled along her spine. ''You—you *wouldn't*.''

His lips twisted in a sly grin that was far from reassuring. ''Watch me.''

CHAPTER FOUR

AFTER Elissa explained about the myth, Alex lifted his chin in a half nod, his expression a mixture of cynicism and amusement. "So..." he said, as though making sure he had all the facts straight, "you're worried your sisters will make something of your being on my property on your birthday?" His lips lifted wryly. "Why? You didn't sleep inside the mansion, did you?"

She hated the way he got right to the heart of the matter. He was like the TV detective, Columbo, who seemed to sense from the first second on the crime scene who the murderer was and then hounded him until he confessed. She bit her tongue to keep from doing just that.

Shaking her head, she lied, "Of course I didn't sleep in the mansion. What an insane question." She had no intention of bringing up anything about the threatening letter she'd received and how it had made her believe she was being stalked that night.

Now that she'd had time to really think about what happened, she realized it was silly to believe someone had known exactly where she would have a flat tire and had been waiting there in the woods for her. The crank letter had spooked her, that was all. The stalker had probably been a deer, the poor animal every bit as startled as she.

Still, Elissa had no plans to go into that or the fact that she'd fulfilled the fable's requirements. The D'Amour myth was nothing more than a fairy tale, and her sister's experiences were charming coincidences. Mentioning it would cause her trouble she didn't need.

Alex pinned her with a dubious look. "I don't quite believe you, Miss Crosby, but…" He stuck his hands into his jeans pockets, the image of a disgruntled male, too good-looking for her peace of mind. Deliberately she shifted her gaze to scan the faded wallpaper. "For now, I'll take your word," he said. "I don't see you as a woman who would sleep inside a deserted mansion in order to snag a husband, then knee the first sucker you meet. It doesn't fit."

She silently thanked heaven that he was buying her story, but the "sucker" remark stung. She spun to glare at him. "Nice talk. What do you have against marriage and families anyway?"

His slow smile became a sneer. "Nothing. It's a fine institution for the terminally self-centered."

Shifting position, Elissa surreptitiously put more distance between them. When he was angry he seemed to take up more space. Unable to understand why her question upset him, she gave a half laugh of impatience. "You should go into the greeting card business, Mr. D'Amour. That's a darling sentiment."

He shrugged, his features solemn. "Do you want to finish your breakfast?"

The question took her off guard. She'd forgotten they'd left Damien and Helen upstairs gaping at their hurried departure. She made a worried face. "What do we tell them we were doing down here?"

He chuckled darkly. "I don't think what we tell them will matter, do you?"

Her exhale was long and dejected. Why didn't some family cancel their reservations so she could get this—this *fly* out of her parlor. As she trudged up the steps beside him, a pessimistic thought intruded. Or was *he* the spider, and was this *his* parlor?

December 23 dawned bright and cold, a brisk north wind ruffling the evergreens and the brown oak leaves clinging to their branches. The rest of the leaf population spiraled and danced over the winter brown lawn, slapping the windows with the urgency of a snowstorm.

The day was passing swiftly and pleasantly, since the guests were all in town taking in the shows and sights. Peace reigned at the inn.

"Oh…" Helen sighed and stretched, drawing Elissa's gaze from her ledger. The youngest of the Crosby sisters stood atop a step stool in the parlor entrance. Elissa couldn't get over how great Helen looked with her ultrashort, ultrafeminine haircut. The style was not only practical for a mother of young twins, but suited Helen's face, making her lovely gray eyes seem large.

"I wish it would snow for Christmas," Helen said as she lay a mistletoe branch over a small hook. Arranging the red ribbon tied in the greenery to its best advantage, she smiled down at her sisters gathered before the fire. Elissa noticed that her glance shifted to her twins, behaving amazingly well as they played with their dolls on the rug. "What's the forecast, Lis?"

"Snow, of course." Smiling, she sat back in the big old leather chair that had been their father's. "I ordered the white stuff, myself. The weatherman and I are just like this." She held up crossed fingers. "Flurries should start sometime Christmas Eve, just in time to give us a full-fledged White Christmas."

Helen backed down the two steps on the stool. "Good. I know how much you spent for those *s-l-e-d-s* you bought for my you-know-who's for you-know-what." With a nod she indicated the towering Christmas tree in the nearby corner, its boughs bright with tiny twinkling lights and Country Christmas ornaments collected from Branson craft shows. Two large sled-shaped packages stood against the wall behind a mountain of smaller presents. "I'd hate to see all that money go to waste."

"It won't," Lucy interjected. "Even if it doesn't snow this year, the you-know-what's will be here for other Christmases. Right, Lis?"

Apprehension stabbed Elissa's heart, but she hid it. She would not allow any negative thoughts to intrude on the holidays. "Absolutely. You don't think I'd let you take them home, do you—I mean how much snow does New York state get?"

Helen laughed. "Oh, right. It's a desert up there—especially in the winter."

The sisters laughed at Helen's joke. Today's newspaper had been plastered with pictures of the wild snowstorm inundating New York at that very moment. "Yes," Elissa said with an emphatic nod. "You're lucky you're here in the Ozark mountains, where we have snow *some* Christmases."

Helen folded the stool. "Now all we have to do is wait for the guys to get back from shopping. And Alex from overseeing construction on his mansion. We can get our Christmas kisses." She gave Elissa a sly look. "*Especially* Alex. I bet you have a hankering to kiss that good-looking hunk. Don't you, Elissa?"

Startled, she shifted to stare at her youngest sister. "What?"

"Or do you already know what it's like to kiss him?"

Elissa could feel her cheeks color. "Now listen, you two." She slapped her ledger book closed in her lap. "Do I have to have it tattooed on my forehead before you'll face the fact that there aren't any sparks of interest between Alex and me. Now, get over it.''

Helen picked up the stool to return it to the pantry. ''Mmm-hmm,'' she said, not sounding convinced.

Lucy shifted to curl her legs beneath her, drawing Elissa's eyes. She gave the blonde a narrowed look. ''You believe me, don't you?''

Lucy smiled. ''Whatever you say.'' She glanced back at her knitting, and took a stitch before she added, ''It's just that you and he are so much alike. You're both ex-lawyers and you're both feisty.''

''Feisty?''

Lucy giggled. ''Helen told me how he practically dragged you out of the dining room the other morning.'' She slanted her older sister a suspicious look. ''What did he want so urgently, anyway, a review of his bill?''

Elissa swallowed. ''It wasn't sexual, if that's what you think.'' She shook her head at Lucy. ''When will you and Helen get it through your heads that I'm not cut out for marriage. I'm argumentative. I'm bullheaded and stubborn...'' She stopped, frowned. ''Or is bullheaded the same thing as stubborn?''

''On you? I'd have to say no,'' came a masculine voice from the parlor entrance. ''The bullheaded Elissa is more painful.''

Both women looked up to see Alex framed in the doorway. He grinned, slipping out of his ski parka and tossing it on a straight-back chair beside the parlor entrance. Elissa watched him, taking in his wide shoulders and the attractive ruddiness of his cheeks, suggesting that he'd walked from the mansion through the woods. His black hair was mussed by the capricious breeze, giving him a country-boy appeal. Dragging her glance away, she checked her watch, feigning boredom. Though she was far from preoccupied with the time, her brain caught the fact that it was five o'clock. Damien and Jack should be back soon.

Just then Helen appeared by his side and Lucy said, "Okay, sister dear, this is your chance to kiss Alex. We expect a full report, don't we Lis?"

Elissa had no idea why Lucy's question embarrassed her. She didn't care if Alex kissed every woman, dog, cat, frog and squirrel in Branson and all of their reports were printed in the newspaper. So why did she feel strangely warm and fluttery at the idea of his kiss? Turning abruptly to thumb through her ledger, she muttered, "Whatever."

"Ah, Helen," Alex said with humor in his tone. "A fantasy come true. However, we must do this fast before jealous husbands show up."

"Too late," Damien called from the front door. "The jealous husbands have arrived."

Alex laughed. "Helen it looks like tradition will have to be served with minimal lust."

Helen giggled. "I'll try to control myself."

"I can't promise the same thing. I'm a wild man when faced with a beautiful woman," Alex teased. "How about a nice, safe handshake?"

"Probably wise," Damien agreed, laughter in his tone.

Helen laughed. "Don't be silly, Alex. We're under the mistletoe. Tradition requires a *kiss*."

"She has a point, Damien," Alex said with a chuckle.

For the next couple of seconds there was no sound, and Elissa pictured Alex taking Helen into his arms. She shook off the image, and concentrated on the figures in her ledger before her. Then she concentrated on them again, battling back visions of Alex crushing Helen against him, devouring her lips in a passionate kiss.

"I give that forehead kiss a perfect ten, Alex. You've done that before, you suave thing."

"I don't want to brag, but yours is not the first forehead I've kissed," he joked.

"Spare me glimpses into your sinful past," Helen teased, "I might swoon."

"No swooning allowed until I've had my turn," came Jack's voice. "Helen, let's have that forehead."

Helen laughed outright this time. "Oh, no, you don't. The forehead is officially Alex's. You can have a cheek—either one. Your choice."

"I had no idea I married such a flirt," Damien interjected, a smile in his voice.

Elissa looked up for this one, watching Jack hug his sister-in-law, as they exchanged cheek kisses. Helen gave him an extra hug of sisterly affection. "I don't know a better cheek-kisser in the entire world, Jack."

With a wink, he stepped back. "My past is every bit as sinful as Alex's."

Helen grinned. "Don't I know it, seeing as I've *slept* with you."

"That's true. Your past is pretty darned sinful, too." Motioning for her husband to come over, he added, "Okay, Damien, your turn. Let's see what she lets *you* kiss."

"Back up a second." Alex broke in, sounding stunned. "You slept with Jack?"

Damien nudged his arm. "Luckily I'm open-minded."

Helen made a face at her husband. "Oh, *sure.*" She smiled at Alex. "I was five years old and afraid of thunder. He was fifteen and called me a scaredy-cat pest."

"Oh." Alex shrugged and put his hands into his pockets, his grin crooked. "For a minute, there, I thought I'd stumbled into some depraved den of iniquity."

Damien hauled his wife into his arms. "I'll see what I can do to arrange that." His voice was husky and meaningful.

"Damien!" Helen squealed with mock consternation. "We're doing cheeks and foreheads!"

"We'll get to those later, sweetheart," Damien mumbled, kissing her with great singleness of mind. Elissa could almost feel the passion they shared, and experienced a surge of envy so strong she was ashamed of herself.

Both Helen and Lucy had quieter, gentler natures than she. Any man who might fall in love with her had his work cut out for him. He'd have to be turned on by a stubborn, smart-mouth who had to beat every opponent into dust. In all her thirty years there hadn't been that many takers, once the awful truth of her personality had come to light. It was odd how men tended not to date a woman who whipped their backsides in law school and who could argue them into mush in the courtroom, and who—face it—even, on a couple of recent occasions, kicked them when they exasperated her beyond words.

"Oh, get a room, you two," Jack admonished with a laugh.

"Luckily they have one," Lucy added.

When the hot kiss finally ended, Damien and Helen stared at each other. Their breathing was heavy, and Helen's cheeks were pink. It was clear something had begun beneath that mistletoe that wasn't over solely because the kiss had ended.

Elissa shook her head at them. "If you two have something pressing to do, we'll watch the girls."

Damien flashed her a grateful look, and without a word, took his wife's hand, leading her toward the stairs.

"Whew." Jack shook his head, looking amused. "It's just a guess, but I think she liked his kiss best." Walking into the parlor, Jack settled on the sofa beside his wife. When he looked at her, his expression was dear. "How are you feeling, Luce?"

She lay her knitting aside and placed a hand on his thigh. Elissa noticed that he covered her hand with his, squeezing gently. She fought back a tear. Love was everywhere in her inn these days. You could cut it like butter. The joy her sisters had found was glorious, filling their lives, making them whole. She struggled not to be jealous of their good fortune.

She tried to be philosophical, reminding herself that some people were meant to be part of a couple, and some weren't. She simply wasn't. She supposed she would have to satisfy herself with mothering them all. That was something, at least, and a role she found gratifying. "Look, you two," she said as gaily as she could, "if you have business elsewhere, I'm perfectly capable of watching the girls for Helen and Damien."

They turned from gazing into each other's eyes and beamed at Elissa. "We're fine," Lucy said. "Besides, we wanted to tell you something—officially."

"About you being pregnant?" Her smile refreshed itself with the reminder. She noticed that Alex was coming into the room and taking a seat on a chair opposite her, before the fire. She avoided looking at him or acknowledging his presence. "I guessed it when you and Jack ran out on breakfast that first morning—and all the oatmeal you've been *not* eating." She reached over and touched her sister's hand. "When's the precious bundle due?"

"Independence Day," Jack said. "Talk about timing."

Elissa clapped her hands together. "It's a sign. Another president in the family." She cast a loving glance at little Elissa Gillian, who was chewing on the foot of her "Feed-and-Wet Frieda" doll. "Of course Gilly will have to be elected to a full two terms, first, but after that, we'll get Baby Gallagher into office." She closed her eyes in feigned rapture. "Of course, I will be secretary of state during both of their terms of office."

"You'll be in a home with a lot of people who think they're Napoleon," Jack laughed.

Elissa eyed him with pretended affront. "Jack Gallagher, do not rain on my presidential parade. I know leadership potential when I see it." She waved a hand at Gilly, gnawing on the doll's leg. "That young lady has presidential timber written all over her."

"She looks more like she has cannibalistic timber to me," Alex interjected.

Elissa looked at him, her features stiffening. "That's not amusing."

Gilly yawned, tossing down her doll. Pushing up, she toddled over to Alex and without preamble slid a knee onto the seat, grabbed a wad of Alex's sweater, and heaved herself into his lap. Before he could react, she'd plopped her head on his chest. With a handful of cashmere gathered into one little fist, she poked her thumb into her mouth.

"Apparently Madam President is going to take a nap," Jack said through a chuckle.

Elissa watched Alex's flummoxed expression as his personal space was invaded by an alien being. He was plainly troubled, but no more so than she. A stab of envy went through her at the sight of her little Gilly snuggling on his lap. It was clear he didn't want the child. Why had her beloved little namesake chosen her arch enemy's lap over her own?

"What do I do?" Alex asked in a whisper as though afraid if he moved the coiled little creature on his belly would strike.

"Don't worry," Jack whispered. "I felt that way the first time I held one of the girls. You get used to it. It's nice, really. Having somebody so tiny and helpless trust you like that." He squeezed Lucy's hand again, glancing her way. "I can't wait for our own."

Jack's reminder that they'd been talking about Lucy's pregnancy brought another question to Elissa's mind. "Does Helen know?"

Lucy laughed. "Oh, yes. After Alex dragged—" She paused and pursed her lips. "I mean, after you and Alex left the table that morning, Helen ran upstairs after me. There wasn't much point in putting off telling her the truth, I couldn't hide my being sick."

Elissa was sorry she'd been so preoccupied with her own troubles that she'd neglected to confirm the wonderful news before now. She tried to smile. "Well, it's the greatest Christmas gift you could give me—*ugh!*" She was suddenly the recipient of a second little body, lumbering into her lap. Big gray eyes gazed up into her own.

"Auntie Lissi?" Glory asked, looking serious.

"Yes, sweetie?"

"Gotta go potty."

"Ah," She took Glory's hands and helped her to the floor. "Well, honey-button, let's go."

As she swept by Alex with her niece in tow, he whispered, "What do I do if this one has to go?"

She eyed him with disdain. "Dial Emergency 911."

When Elissa and Glory returned to the parlor, Lucy and Jack were gathering up a limp little Gilly from Alex's lap.

"What's going on?" Elissa asked.

"We decided to take a walk with the twins," Lucy said. "I don't think Helen wants Gilly taking a nap now and then staying up until all hours."

Elissa nodded. "Good thinking." She bent to talk to Glory. "Honey, you and Auntie Lucy and Uncle Jack are going for a walk. Will you bring me back some pinecones for a centerpiece?"

Glory's expressive little face screwed up. "Piecone?"

Lucy took her hand. "Sure, sweetie. You have them at mommy's and daddy's house. I'll show you what they are, to remind you. We'll get a sack in the kitchen."

"Their coats are in the closet under the stairs."

"Check," Jack called as he left the parlor, hoisting Gilly in an arm. "Come on Gilly, wake up."

"Juice?" Gilly asked sleepily, rubbing an eye with a chubby fist.

"Sure we'll get some juice. After we walk."

Elissa noticed movement outside the parlor window, and was happy to see the mail truck lumbering along the road. She watched as it stopped at their box. "Finally," she mumbled. "The mail's getting later and later."

"It's Christmas," Alex said, still sitting in the easy chair beside the fireplace.

She jerked to look at him, having momentarily been able to put his existence from her mind. "Wow, there's news," she said sarcastically, spinning toward the door. "Christmas—a busy time for the post office. Who would have thought?"

"Use my jacket if you want," he called.

She realized it was stupid to go out with the temperature below freezing, so she spun back. Stiff-jawed, she muttered, "Thank you," grabbing up the ski parka.

He nodded, then turned to stare into the fire.

She slipped into his coat. It was huge, but warm. And it held his tobacco-cedar scent. She snuggled deep into the collar when the cold wind hit her face, inhaling him with a combination of regret and guilty pleasure. He smelled good for a sleazy, property-stealing rat.

Though it was rapidly growing dark, the sunset was fiery and breathtaking. She inhaled the cold evening air—and Alex's scent—and found herself smiling. She decided the smile was for the crisp, fresh air and the striking sunset, and that was all.

She had a feeling the walk Lucy and Jack and the twins were taking out back in the woods would be short. But it would certainly wake up Gilly. The cold air was exhilarating.

Thumbing through the mail on her way back to the house, she saw *it* and staggered to a halt. This is what she had feared. Another smudged envelope with the same irregular scrawl. Her name, her address, in that heavy-handed brown ink. Just like the first letter.

Her hands began to tremble, and she dropped half the mail. Envelopes began to blow around the yard, but she hardly saw it, didn't care. "Oh…" she cried, her voice a quivery whisper. "Oh, no." Tearing the thing open, she forced herself to read the coarse scribble.

Don't have you too happy a christmas, missy. I'm watching yu and I'm going to have my rivenge. You don't got no chance to excape. See yu real soon, missy. But yu won't see me coming.

Of course it wasn't signed. She didn't expect it to be. She scanned the postmark. Kissie, Missouri, a small town not far away. The other had been postmarked from Hollister, another nearby town. Maybe this creep had been lurking in the woods that night she'd hidden in the D'Amour mansion, after all. Maybe somebody really was stalking her. He could have put the board in the road with the nails in it just so she would have her flat tire right there. Just so that he—

"Elissa, what's wrong?" came a concerned voice, not far away. "From the window I saw you turn as white as a sheet."

She shot a gaze at the tall man standing there coatless, watching her closely. For several seconds she was too affected to move, captured against her will by his arresting presence. For the blink of an eye, the crimson flame of the sunset gave him a radiant halo and he looked too perfect to be mortal. A thickness came to her throat, cutting off her ability to speak.

"Elissa?" he repeated softly, as though afraid she might panic and scream if he spoke too loudly. "What is it?"

Pulled from her trance, she didn't say anything—had no intention of involving him in her private life. She shook her head emphatically, hoping this letter would give police the clue they needed to find this lowlife before he decided to do something besides write letters. "It's nothing," she muttered. Angered that Alex had been watching from the window, butting in to something that wasn't his business, she spun away, fumbling along the ground for the wind-tossed mail. "Are you going to help or just stand there cross-examining me?"

She heard his guttural curse, then watched out of the corner of her eye as he moved off to chase envelopes along the side of the house. By the time he was back with the mail, she had her story worked out.

"Sick friend," she mumbled, stuffing the offending envelope into her suit jacket pocket. "It's sad to be in hospital during Christmas."

He handed her the rest of her mail, his expression skeptical. "You're a lousy liar, Miss Crosby."

That did it! She thrust out her chin, hoping her quarrelsome bravado would be enough to get him to back off. "And you're a nosy trespasser who needs to learn to mind his own business."

"Is it from your lawyer friend? Is it the proof of my ownership?"

She glared at him for another second, then stomped by. "Right. The whole world revolves around you and your business!" As an afterthought, she shrugged out of his coat and turned back to toss it at him. He snagged it as it sailed toward his face, his frown more concerned than angry. "Egotism is the last refuge of the scoundrel, you know!" she shouted.

"Whatever the hell that means," he grumbled.

Quivery with rage, and the nagging torment of the sinister letters, she sprinted away.

Did Alex D'Amour own her inn? Was she going to lose everything? And if there really was a nutcase out there bent on some crazy revenge, did that mean she might lose her life, too?

She swallowed hard around the lump of dread blocking her throat.

CHAPTER FIVE

IN THE dead of night, during the wee hours of Christmas day, Elissa was awakened by a sound. She lay motionless in her bed, listening. What was it? Scratching? No. It sounded more like something scraping against wood. She heard it again and bolted upright, her adrenaline pumping blood through her veins as if it were a freight train running through a tunnel. Her ears roared with the unfamiliar noise and her heart nearly leapt from her chest. Someone was trying to break into the narrow basement window above her bed.

With a cry, she sprang from the covers and vaulted toward her door, dragging blankets and sheets as she fled. Banging the door shut behind her, she sprinted toward the stairs in the total darkness, only to smash into a solid object that shouldn't have been there. She shrieked, positive a gang of thugs had invaded the place, bent on heaven only knew what horrible crimes.

She reflexively shot up a knee, but her target deftly moved, and her hands were clutched in a tight grasp. "Whoa," came a sleepy, but familiar, male voice. "What's this? Surprise attacks at night, now?"

When she realized the man who held her wasn't a murderer or rapist, but another lowlife she had on her hands, she fell against him in an effort to push him toward the exit. "Somebody's breaking into my room," she wheezed. "We have to get out of here!"

"Somebody's breaking into your room?" he asked, this time in a concerned whisper. She had a feeling he was frowning, but it was too dark to be sure. "Hell." Releasing her, he headed for her bedroom.

"No!" She yanked on the back of his shorts. "Are you crazy?"

Brushing away her hand he opened the door slightly. "Any self-respecting robber would be long gone by now, once he heard that door bang shut."

She scurried up behind him, needing the security of a strong human being nearby. Her hands fluttered to his shoulders and held on. Through her fingertips she could feel taut muscle, and knew he was tensed for a fight. She peered around him. "See anything?"

"No." He started to step into the room, and she grasped his upper arm. "Don't go in there, he might have a gun."

The lights flashed on. A scream of terror rose to Elissa's lips, but died there, as she realized it had been Alex's doing, not a night-blind gunman.

When Alex stepped inside the room, she did, too, preferring his nearness to the basement parlor teeming with shadows. She was ashamed of herself for acting like a child. This was completely unlike her. Apparently the threatening letters had spooked her more than she realized.

She'd taken the second letter to the police yesterday, and was assured they would do their best to find the culprit. But she knew that Christmas time in Branson was a busy one for everybody, including the police. She doubted that two crank letters would get top priority. She'd also taken in a list of past legal clients who might have a grudge against her. Once again, she was assured they would do everything possible to get to the bottom of it.

Alex stepped up on her bed and examined the window. "It hasn't been opened. This window's painted shut."

"I—I did that last summer."

He turned to look down at her as she huddled near the foot of the bed. Towering there, all California tan and muscle, he seemed like a Greek god, come to earth. She wondered what the name of the Greek god of mattresses might be, because if there wasn't one, she certainly had a candidate standing in front of her. Hopping off the bed, he scanned her, his expression concerned. "You're pale. Are you going to faint?"

She felt a twinge of shame at the question and straightened her shoulders. "No, I'm not going to faint." Gulping in a breath to fight her light-headedness, she manufactured a calm facade. "I was startled, that's all." She backpedaled, trying to sound unruffled. "Being awakened out of a sound sleep can be frightening."

"Are you sure it wasn't a dream?" Alex asked, concern etching his features.

She felt stupid and shook her head. "No—no, I'm not sure." Suddenly she felt very silly. "I guess I'm just goosey about the—" She bit off her statement, wincing at what she'd almost let slip. "I mean—sometimes dreams can seem very real. That's all."

His features didn't exhibit much faith in her story about a dream, and he turned to confront her. "Do you have dreams of people breaking into your room often?"

His sarcasm irritated her. "My dreams are none of your business."

"Except when you come screaming into my arms. That makes them my business."

She looked away, embarrassed, and counted to ten. She didn't want to fight and she was sure the more fuss she made, the more suspicious Alex would get. After all, she probably had been dreaming. What she heard—or thought she heard—was very likely a fabrication of her overstressed mind. The last thing she wanted to do was ruin Christmas for her family.

When she looked at Alex again, she shrugged, working to appear nonchalant. "I'm sorry about overreacting, Mr. D'Amour. Let's just forget the whole thing, okay? At worst, a possum was trying to get in out of the cold."

His steady interrogator's gaze was too intent for her peace of mind and she had to force herself not to fidget. She toyed with the idea of giving the police a quick call later. But because she'd brandished a letter opener, accusing Alex of attacking her—in front of three shocked policemen—she would probably need concrete proof that something was amiss this time, or they might decide to label her as a kook and stop taking her case seriously. She didn't want to chance that.

Cocking his head in a gesture that said he didn't buy her story, Alex prodded, "What are you hiding? First that letter that frightened the wits out of you the other day and now, people breaking into your room?"

"Nobody broke into my room!" she snapped. "Get off that!" Stalking away from him, she caught a glimpse of herself in the mirror over her dresser and stumbled to a halt. She was actually prancing around in front of this man in nothing but an oversize green T-shirt.

Tugging at the garment in a vain effort to magically make it longer, she watched her face color with embarrassment. Swiping nervous hands through her hair, she turned her back on him. "Look, don't you think it's possible I might be upset because of your attempt to pirate my property?" Improvising, she hurried on, "Maybe the break-in nightmare was about *you* and your attempt to steal my inn, did you ever think of that?" She whirled on him, a triumphant surge going through her. That should shut him up.

His features were drawn in a provoked frown. "The property was stolen from me, Miss Crosby." His jaws worked and Elissa had a feeling that, this time, he was counting to ten. Visibly perturbed, he looked away, mumbling, "I told you I'd reimburse you for any improvements you've made. You know I'm not legally bound to do so. What more do you expect of me?"

His glance met hers again and she was struck by the eerie beauty of his silver eyes, his temper transforming them into a force of nature all their own. "The eighth wonder of the world" flitted through her mind, but she swept the thought away as quickly as it came.

Incensed that she allowed herself to be drawn to him, she jabbed a finger toward her bedroom door. "Would you leave? I have to get dressed."

His expression grew puzzled. "Dressed?" He looked at his wristwatch. "It's four o'clock in the morning. Even Bella doesn't arrive for another hour and a half."

She moved to the door and pointedly held it wide. "I have to start the Christmas turkey. Dad always smoked it on the charcoaler, and I intend to carry on the tradition—*if* it's any of your business."

Alex's eyebrows rose in apparent surprise. "A Renaissance woman. Is there anything you can't do?"

She was taken aback by the compliment but refused to be affected. He'd probably been mocking her, anyway. "Apparently I can't get men out of my bedroom," she countered.

His lips quirked for a split second before his expression turned serious. "I can see where that could become troubling." With a nod that was almost courtly, he left her to her privacy.

Once the door clicked shut she breathed a sigh of relief that he hadn't made a more insulting joke out of her badly worded retort. Such as, "You're lucky you can get any men *in* your bedroom," or something equally cutting—since he'd made it clear that he thought of her as a love-starved old maid.

Sinking to her bed, she put her hands over her face. She had more serious problems than Alex D'Amour's opinion of her love life. Her mind churned. Had what she'd thought she'd heard really been a bad dream brought on by Alex's threat to take away her inn, or had somebody actually tried to break in?

She didn't want to think about it. Of course, if it had been a break-in attempt, it might have been unrelated to the letters. After all, it was a well-known fact that thieves loved to break in at Christmas time to steal all the goodies from under the tree. If that were the case, then her scream and the slamming of the door had foiled the plan and it was all over.

She decided to let it go, this time, and not bother the police. Ninety-nine chances out of a hundred, the sound she'd heard had been nothing even remotely ominous. After all, it was Christmas. Dawn was coming. Why make a fool of herself by crying wolf, again? This was a joyous holiday and shouldn't be spoiled with irrational worries.

Glancing at her bedside clock she realized that if she didn't get that turkey on, they'd be eating raw bird for their Christmas dinner instead of a juicy, smoked turkey. Hustling into a pair of black wool slacks and an oversize red sweater Lucy had knitted for her birthday, Elissa headed out of the basement and up into the kitchen only to find the lights on and Alex standing there, looking yummy in jeans and a dove gray cashmere pullover.

"What do you think you're doing?" She shifted her glance from his bothersome eyes to his neck. He exuded a sexy power that attracted her, and she fought it with a prickly attitude.

He shrugged. "I figured since I'm going to be a gentleman land owner, I should learn to charcoal meat. I hear it's a popular pastime in the Midwest."

She met his gaze with resentment. "And you think I'll teach you?"

Those wide shoulders lifted and fell again. "I thought you might." His lips crooked in a wily grin, revealing unsettling dimples. "Especially since it's dark outside and that—possum could still be around."

She experienced an inner shudder at the reminder of what had sent her barreling into his arms not long before. She hated to admit it, but Alex D'Amour's massive presence might be advantageous. Swallowing, she spun toward the cabinet where she kept the lighter fluid and matches. "Uh, the bag of charcoal's in the pantry storeroom."

Without looking directly into those astute eyes, she led him through to the front of the inn. They grabbed their coats from the closet under the stairs, then went out the front door and around to the side veranda where the charcoal grill was kept. "All right," she muttered grudgingly, "stack the charcoal in the grill."

"Okay, professor," he murmured, very near.

As he poured and stacked the coals, Elissa noticed twinkling flakes of snow in the light that spilled from the porch into the darkness. *It was snowing.* Moving to the rail, she watched the flakes drift down, silent and lovely.

"What do you see?" Alex asked, sounding wary.

She grinned into the darkness. "It's okay. It's just snowing."

She heard his footfalls as he joined her at the railing. "Growing up in California, I never saw snow except when we went skiing in Colorado over Christmas."

"We?" She peered at him, finding herself needing to know about his family. "That sounds like a nice way to spend the holidays. Do you have brothers and sisters?"

He looked at her, his features suddenly grim. "No." Abruptly he turned away, stomping back to scan the charcoals, still blazing and far from ready for the turkey.

Elissa faced him, leaning on the rail. "Did your parents take you skiing every Christmas?"

He grinned, but there was no humor in the show of teeth. "My parents? No, Miss Crosby, they didn't." When he lifted his gaze to hers, his eyes revealed a flame that Elissa sensed was from an inner vehemence rather than the burning charcoal. "Let's just say we weren't close."

Clearly he didn't intend to expand on the subject, and Elissa tried to convince herself that she didn't care one way or the other. But she couldn't quite manage it. For a fraction of a second she'd seen something vulnerable in his eyes, and the memory haunted her.

The snow was coming harder, now, and it was evident they would have a white Christmas. Though Elissa was standing out on her veranda with her worst enemy, her spirits lifted a notch. What could be more picture-perfect than a snowy Christmas with lots of good food and a close family sharing the joys of the holiday? She smiled wistfully at the vision, struggling to push away her fear.

"It's really coming down," Alex said, bringing her back. She was surprised to see that he was beside her again, his hands resting on the railing as he watched the snow twirl and dance, thicker, ever thicker, a ballet of heavenly scraps of lace.

In a self-protective move, she leaned away from him. Resting her shoulder against a support pole, she peeked at his profile. The veranda light emphasized his prominent cheekbones and bore witness to his skin, attractively rosy with the cold. On his wind-mussed hair a few wayward snowflakes had made their home, twinkling as if they were fallen stars. Uneasy with the way the sight made her go all fluttery inside, she shifted away, lifting her hands to her own curls. She could feel the damp, coldness of snowflakes that had settled there. Shaking her head, she smoothed her hair back.

"Why did you do that?" he asked, startling her, for she hadn't realized he'd been watching. "Your hair's amazing with snow gleaming in it. Like red coral, just under the surface of a sunlit sea."

She felt a foolish tingle at his hushed remark and lowered her gaze. If he thought she'd give up her fight for her property because of a few pretty words, he was crazy. "Enough snow in your hair and you catch pneumonia." Plodding to the grill, she glared down at the glowing coals.

"You have so much stubborn pride, Elissa, you can't even take a compliment from me?" he asked as he joined her.

She glared at him. "It's an ugly flaw, I know." The Christmas spirit draining from her, she bit out the words, "Imagine me not swooning under such praise about my hair—when all you want from me is my entire life!"

"That's not fair—"

"*Turkey!*" she blurted, needing to change the subject.

His expression grew wry. "Is it time to cook the bird, or are you talking about me?"

She wheeled away, heading for the front door, the hollow thud of her footsteps loud in the morning stillness.

Elissa watched Alex with reluctant fascination. He was a wildly successful, sophisticated lawyer, yet he'd obviously never been involved in a family Christmas. He'd never seen children playing before a wood fire, never opened Christmas packages at dawn, or watched football while women laughed and cooked in the next room— every so often calling for one of the men to "check the turkey and turn down the TV."

She couldn't help laughing at him when he checked his watch at one o'clock, suggesting they should have put the turkey on earlier, since lunch was already an hour late. She didn't know why she took such delight in telling him that "noon" on Christmas day really meant about three o'clock. He'd actually been surprised with the news. Alex D'Amour was like an alien dropped down from Planet Humbug, where holidays were not celebrated. Or maybe he was more like some recently manufactured android with no knowledge of kin or customs.

His surprise about so many things they took for granted touched something in her, and that shocked her. She found herself wondering where this man had spent his formative Christmases? She was even more stunned to realize she was harboring some uncharitable thoughts for the people who *hadn't* taught him about rising at dawn full of expectation, of eating homemade cinnamon rolls and drinking eggnog for breakfast. Of sitting around a roaring fire, eating turkey and dressing off paper plates, while watching toddlers ignore their gifts to play with the boxes.

Several of the inn's guests had opted to stay in out of the snow and eat Christmas Dinner at the inn, so there was lots of clamor and laughter. By five o'clock things had quieted down. Bella and Ramona had cleaned away the Christmas meal debris and left for celebrations of their own. Even the least adventuresome guests had braved the snow to go into town to see much anticipated Christmas shows, featuring America's biggest music stars.

The twins were asleep, exhausted. Christmas music played softly in the background and the scent of wood smoke and Christmas tree pine filled the air. Lucy was curled up on the parlor couch, knitting something tiny and yellow.

Her glance drifted to Glory who was sound asleep, stretched out on a blanket before the fire, her head half inside the box her Barbie Pet Doctor doll had come in. The Veterinarian Barbie's toes were pressed against her cherubic mouth. With a rush of tenderness, Elissa decided her niece looked like a little doll herself.

Her gaze roamed to the chair opposite her own, where Alex sat. His eyes were closed and one arm was wrapped around Gilly, who seemed to have decided that Alex and his cashmere chest was just about the greatest napping spot in the world. The toddler was dribbling all over the expensive sweater. She twitched in her sleep, her little fist grabbing another wad of cashmere. As she readjusted her backside, cuddled in Alex's big hand, his long fingers moved, shifted to better accommodate her. Elissa's lips twitched at the toddler's assumption that she was right at home on this stranger's lap. She decided she'd have to keep an eye on that young lady—a natural coquette.

Elissa scanned Alex's hand, cupping Gilly's hips. His

nails were neatly trimmed, his fingers graceful, gentle. Ringless. She winced, wondering where that thought had come from. She had absolutely no interest in his romantic attachments. Her gaze trailing up to his face, she worked to repair her thinking—reminding herself that this man was an ogre as far as she was concerned.

Watching him, she found herself wondering if he was sleeping or simply resting his eyes. For a man who had never had anything to do with babies, he was being a pretty good sport about Gilly. Facing that difficult fact put a small rip in the fabric of her dislike for him.

She gritted her teeth, trying to shake off the resurgence of soft emotion. What was it about this man who could allow himself to be a mattress for a tiny little thing like Gilly, and at the same time so heartlessly try to take away everything she'd worked for these last four years? She lowered her glance to her fisted hands, her emotions suddenly conflicted. She didn't like this irreconcilable mix of feelings. She preferred harboring pure, unadulterated loathing for the man.

A noise from the front door drew Elissa's attention in time to see Damien, Jack and Helen come inside, shedding coats, laughing about who won the three-way snowball fight. Elissa lifted a finger to her lips, cautioning in a loud whisper, "We have sleeping babies in here."

The three intrepid warriors grew hushed and peeked into the parlor. "Maybe we'd better take them up to bed," Helen whispered to Damien. "I think we'll owe Alex for about ten cashmere sweaters if we're not careful." She walked over to pick up a limp little Gilly, and smiled at Alex. "I hope she isn't too much of a bother. Honestly I have no idea why she's so attached to sleeping on you."

Alex grinned. "I have that effect on some women. They see me and fall asleep."

Elissa eyed him dubiously, knowing that was a lie. But she also knew that any comment to the contrary would take her where she didn't want to go.

Helen laughed, snuggling Gilly to her. "I would imagine the only women you affect that way are under three years old." She passed Elissa a sly look, but thankfully kept any further thoughts to herself.

Damien scooped up Glory. "Well, folks, we'll see you later. I think it's time for a family nap."

Lucy stretched, laying her knitting in her bag. "I'm for that. I can hardly keep my eyes open."

Jack came over to the sofa and took her hand. "Good idea." He looked at Alex and then Elissa as he tucked Lucy under a protective arm. "We'll see you later."

Elissa nodded, deciding she needed a nap, too. Unfortunately, since she didn't have time for such luxuries, the next most important thing she needed to do was leave the room. She had no desire to be left alone with Alex. She stood. "Well, if everybody else is going to desert me, I guess I'll go work on my accounts."

As she passed Alex's chair, he caught her wrist. With a frown of confusion she stared at him, but couldn't speak.

"It was nice, today," he said. "Thank you."

Jarred by his compliments, she continued to stare at him, her emotions at war. After a few seconds, she pulled from his grasp. "Now you can smoke a turkey. Big deal."

He winced slightly at her curtness. "Look, I'm not your enemy."

She swallowed hard. "If it makes you feel better to think that, Mr. D'Amour..." She couldn't go on. But there was no need. The flash in his eyes told her the message had been received.

He rose from the chair and she took that as her cue to leave—to escape to her office and get out from under the heat of his gaze. When she reached the parlor door, she remembered she'd left the shawl Lucy had knitted for her for Christmas and hurried back to snatch it up.

This time when she got to the parlor entrance, Alex was standing there. She breezed past, but he caught her hand. "I'm standing under the mistletoe, Miss Crosby."

"My middle name is Gardenia," she retorted. "Now that we've exchanged holiday trivia, let me—"

Go! That had been the word she'd almost said. Unhappily, as her lips opened to say it, his mouth closed over hers, shocking her into stillness. A strange, almost imperceptible tremor went through her as his lips took hers captive. His kiss was wildly masculine, stealing her breath. As his mouth moved over hers, she struggled to tame an urge to wrap her arms around his neck and draw him against her.

She tried to protest, wanted to, but her voice wouldn't come. And even though he was still holding one of her hands, the other was free—free to shove against his chest, to make it clear she didn't want this. Yet, that hand didn't resist. Instead she found herself drifting toward him, her fingers whispering along his cheek in a caress, then slipping back to stroke the hair at his nape. So soft. And his scent—so stirring.

Though her mind was numbed by his provocative kiss, Elissa still managed to seize on an irony. She'd had several marriage proposals in her life, rejecting them in favor of her precious independence. But with this offensive man's kiss she felt strangely uncertain, her need for self-rule undermined in some insidious way.

His hand moved to cup her waist, warm, big and *welcome*, tugging her into him. She heard a ragged whimper of need escape her throat—a sound she'd never heard before. It frightened her, brought her back to reality as surely as if a snowball had been thrown in her face.

Though some crazy part of her experienced a reluctance to be separated from him, she yanked at his hold and shoved against his chest, stumbling a step away when he released her. "You—you…" she exclaimed in a husky exhale. "Never do that again!"

He grinned. "Merry Christmas to you, too, Gardenia. And thanks for the tie."

"I didn't give you any tie," she cried, her lips throbbing. "Helen and Lucy must have done it and put my name on it." Taking a protective step away, she poked a finger toward his chest. "And if you ever call me Gardenia again, I'll—I'll…"

"Knee me?" His grin was outrageously sexy, those dimples taunting, making her heart jump foolishly. "Funny you didn't think of doing it when I kissed you." With that telling remark, he walked away, leaving Elissa fairly sure she was coming down with some terrible flu. She was shaky…feverish…short of breath. And her lips were swollen. Swollen and sizzling! That had to be bad. Squeezing her eyes shut, she slumped against the door jamb, her mind shrieking, *Yes—dear heaven—please let it be the flu.*

CHAPTER SIX

THAT evening, Elissa discovered to her amazement that she was hungry, and went upstairs to make a turkey sandwich. She wasn't surprised to find someone there ahead of her, but was grateful it was Helen, not Alex. Her sister explained that the rest of the family and a few guests—as well as Mr. Inn Stealer—were in the parlor enjoying the warm fire and a friendly chat.

Helen was slicing turkey. "We were taking bets on when you'd come up for air." She smiled. "You know, Lis, it's not healthy to spend so much time underground. People will think you're a mole."

Elissa managed a weak grin. "Well, I'm a starving mole." She pulled up a chair and slathered mustard on the wheat bread Helen had laid out. She laughed wryly. "This afternoon I thought I would never be able to eat again."

Helen handed her the plate of sliced turkey, then drew up a chair beside her at the table. "You need lots of energy."

There was something odd in Helen's tone, and Elissa looked her way. "What do you mean?"

Helen leaned closer, though there was nobody within earshot. "For your wild love affair with Alex."

Elissa stilled, unable to believe her ears. "Are you insane?"

Helen took the mustard knife from her sister's limp hand and began to apply the condiment to another piece of bread. "Don't be coy, Lis. It's as plain as your flaming red hair that you've met your match.'' She nudged Elissa's shoulder. ''Now you have somebody you can argue with to your heart's content. I've heard it's the only way lawyers can have orgasms—arguing themselves into a state of sexual euphoria.''

Elissa knew her jaw had gone slack, but she couldn't seem to do anything about it. She could only gape at her sister, aghast. Where had the shy little protector of broken animals gone? Who was this woman glibly discussing lawyers and their orgasms?

Seemingly unperturbed, Helen went back to making sandwiches. ''It's too bad you've already had your birthday, or I'd suggest you go take a nap in the mansion.'' She peered at Elissa, her expression teasing. ''I'd use my charming personality to entice Alex over there the first thing in the morning and—well, let nature take its course.'' She prodded her sister suggestively with her elbow.

The impact helped bring Elissa back, her temper flaring. She tried to squelch it. After all, hadn't she taken great pains to make sure her sisters didn't know her true feelings about Alex D'Amour. ''Don't be silly,'' she snapped, then forced her tone to be more neutral. ''Alex and I are just acquaintances. To be honest, I find him— utterly—resistible.''

Helen's smile faded for an instant before it was refreshed. She chuckled. ''For a second there I almost believed you.'' Standing, she indicated a platter of sandwiches that had somehow been thrown together while Elissa was in her trance. ''But your actions speak louder than your words.''

Elissa vaulted up. ''What actions?'' She'd had to force herself several times not to jump the man bodily and pummel him into the ground. Maybe she shouldn't have bothered being so discreet.

Helen picked up the platter. "You look at him *all* the time. Your eyes say things."

"No they don't!" Elissa dogged her sister's heels as she headed toward the kitchen door. "My eyes haven't even given the *slightest* thought to that man!"

"What man?" came a deep voice. Both women stumbled to a halt when Alex appeared in the kitchen's entrance.

Helen walked up to him, placing the plate of sandwiches in his hands. "Look who's here, Elissa." She turned, wagging her brows. "Why, it's Alex D'Amour— of all people."

Elissa decided that if her eyes were ever going to communicate anything, it had to be now. She telegraphed a message to Helen that screamed, *Keep your mouth shut!* Though the communication was just short of lethal, Helen laughed merrily, taking Alex's arm and steering him toward the parlor. "Now what were we talking about?"

"Some man?" he offered.

"Oh?" As they left, Helen tilted her head at him, her expression believably quizzical. "My mind's a blank."

Once they'd gone, Elissa sank into a chair, relieved that Helen had obeyed her wordless order. Where had her sister gotten such a ridiculous idea?

She fiddled absently with the mustard bottle, her mind running back over what Helen had said about the myth. Though she loved her baby sister with all her heart, that didn't change the fact that she was an idealistic dreamer. The myth was nothing more than pretty words. The fact that both her younger sisters had met their husbands the way the myth suggested they would was mere coincidence. Bizarre, maybe, but a coincidence, nevertheless.

Gritting her teeth, she renewed her vow that she would *never* let anyone find out that she'd actually slept in the mansion on her birthday—and that the intolerable Alex D'Amour had been the first man she'd seen that morning. Her sisters were bad enough with their conniving glances and innuendoes, now. If they found out the truth, she would be put in an unbearable position. Her nerves were tattered enough having Alex D'Amour underfoot— a constant reminder that he intended to take away her livelihood.

She heard a pop and discovered she'd cracked the glass jar with her tight grip. Placing trembling fingers to her lips, she winced at the bitter taste of mustard and blood.

The day after Christmas, Damien and Helen took the girls out to the side yard to hang strings of suet, for the birds, in a cedar tree. Lucy wasn't feeling well, so she and Jack were upstairs in their room. Early that morning, Alex had trekked off in the snow toward his mansion. The inn's guests had scattered for the day.

After finishing with the morning's business, Elissa came upstairs and heard the familiar grumble of the mail truck's engine. She was pleased to note that it was arriving earlier, since the pre-Christmas madness was over. She tromped through the fluffy three-inch snowfall to retrieve that day's delivery.

Though the thought flitted through her mind that another sinister letter might be among late Christmas cards, bills and junk mail, she forced the idea from her mind. With a friendly greeting to the postman, she accepted the stack of envelopes.

He pulled away, his 'happy new year' half buried beneath the clanking protest of his truck's acceleration.

She turned toward the inn, thumbing through the mail. Even before she recognized the messy scrawl, the short hairs on her nape stood up. Though she went weak all over, she managed not to drop everything in the snow.

A shrill laugh invaded her fear-cloaked mind, and she realized the girls were running around on the front lawn. Knowing Damien and Helen would be following, she panicked that her expression would give away trouble. Swerving, she headed around the opposite side of the house, intent on entering by the back door.

Once she reached the steps that led to the kitchen, she couldn't stand it any longer. Laying the other mail aside, she tore open the letter. Dread thundered through her as she read, and she dropped to the bottom step. This one was worse than the others.

Missy, don't plan on having no happy new year. You ain't gonna have one.

Terror made her shiver. Something in the ominous wording smacked of a threat on her life. If this letter-writing turned out to be nothing more than a joke, then it was a very sick one.

She turned the envelope over. This letter had been postmarked in Branson. She ran a hand through her hair. *So what?* She scolded silently. Whoever he was, he was probably too cowardly to really do anything. Yet even as her rational side counseled with her panicking side, she trembled uncontrollably.

"*Ohmigod,* another one?"

Her head jerked up to see Alex trekking her way. His cheeks were aglow, his raven hair wind-tossed. His long legs seemed even longer in the form-fitting jeans and thick-soled boots. Shoulders swathed in a down-filled parka, took on an epic width. His breath frosted the air as if it were smoke, and his scowl was so deep he seemed to be some mythical man-dragon charging out of his forest lair.

She closed her eyes, mortified that he always seemed to sneak up on her when she was most vulnerable. Angry with herself for being too weak-willed to get to the privacy of her office before she opened the damnable letter, she took it out on him. "Will you *please* mind your own business?"

The crunch of his boots told her he was close. She even detected his aftershave in the cold air. Unable to help herself, she peered at him the instant he leaned down, plucking the letter from her lap. She grabbed at it, managing to snatch it away. "Just because you think you own my inn doesn't mean you have any business reading my mail," she hissed, aware that Damien and Helen were outside and might hear if she spoke too loudly.

Gathering up the rest of her mail, she twisted around to go inside. As she took the first step away from him a black, ugly thought struck her square between the eyes and she halted. *"Oh my Lord."* She exhaled in a moan, turning to glare at him. "Or is this particular piece of mail *your* business?"

He stared at her, appearing confused.

Suddenly it all made sense. His arrival shortly after the first threatening letter. Then believing she'd been stalked that night she'd had a flat tire, plus the fact that Alex had been right there the next morning. And now these two other letters arriving while he was staying in her inn. *It was all Alex's doing!*

It would have been easy for him to ask one of the workers to take a letter home with instructions to mail it from some nearby town. *"You!"* She glared at him, raging inside.

"What are you—"

"If you can't get rid of me legally, you'll ice the cake with some intimidation! I see it all now!" she whispered angrily. "By threatening my life your plan was to frighten me out of here!"

His eyes widened. "Somebody's threatened your life?"

He asked the question in such hushed amazement that Elissa found it hard to believe he was pretending. Before she could react to his question, he was grasping her by the arms. Startled by the move, she allowed the mail to fall, unheeded, into the snow.

"Hell, Elissa. Why? Why would anyone want to harm you?" His eyes held her hostage for a long moment, and she thought she saw distress there. Or did she? Was he that adept at showing precisely the emotion he wanted to express? She already knew he was a master at playing a part. Maybe he was merely acting the innocent to take her off her guard.

Uncomfortable with the rush of—of some unnamable emotion she felt when she looked into those eyes, she jerked from his grasp. "I only know one person who wants me out of the way—and that's you, Mr. D'Amour." Forgetting the mail, she turned and ran up the steps. "You do the math."

"That's not the way I operate, Miss Crosby," he growled.

As she escaped to her basement office, his words soaked in. *That's not the way I operate.* Though she didn't want to admit it, she supposed it was true. Mr.

Alex D'Amour—nationally celebrated lawyer—was a man with a tremendous ego. He would naturally assume he could win any legal fight he embarked upon by the golden brilliance of his arguments. His self-assurance would never allow him to threaten anyone with anonymous letters.

As she tossed her coat onto her filing cabinet, she faced the fact that Alex wasn't responsible. It was simply the timing of the two separate occurrences that had sent her mind spiraling along that path.

Dropping into her chair, she covered her face with her hands, wishing she could enjoy the luxury of a good cry, but knowing she couldn't, didn't dare let her guard down. She was afraid if she did she'd become a screaming, jibbering wreck.

But if not Alex, then who was writing these ghastly letters? Even if it was nothing more than a prank conjured up in some perverted mind, it came at a terrible time. She couldn't take much more.

Hearing a noise, she looked up to see Alex lay the mail on her desk, the threatening letter on top. It was unfolded, a clear indication that he'd read it. She chanced a peek at his face, grim, his eyes on her. "You don't really think I sent this, do you?" he asked, almost too softly to be heard.

With a sinking feeling in the pit of her stomach, she shook her head. "No—I—I'm sorry..."

"I'm calling the police."

When he reached for the phone, she stilled his hand. "This isn't your concern, Alex. Besides, people who write these kinds of letters are too cowardly to really *do* anything."

"Where the hell did you hear that?"

She blanched, but forged on with her bluff. "It's—

common knowledge. Statistics…'' In the face of his cynical gaze she couldn't go on.

''When do you want me to call the police, after you're a statistic?''

With a heavy sigh she broke eye contact. ''That's not funny.''

''Damned straight.''

She heard him lift the receiver and slammed her hand on top of his. ''Don't bother,'' she said through a weary sigh. ''I've already called the police. They're working on the case.'' She squeezed his hand, her expression pleading. ''Promise me you'll keep this to yourself. I won't have my family's holiday spoiled by something that's nothing but a sick joke.''

He held on to the receiver, his glance stormy, his jaw working. ''I've never met such a hardheaded woman in my life,'' he muttered. ''Damn.''

She experienced an ironic sense that she'd been complimented, and she smiled wearily. ''Thanks.'' She indicated the door with a nod. ''Now go away. It's under control, okay?''

Her hand was still clamped over his on the phone receiver. She knew if he wanted to, he could easily throw her off, so she had the impression that he was rethinking the whole thing, too.

''All right, Miss Crosby.'' He lifted his hand from the phone and ran it through his hair. ''As long as you keep the police informed.'' He shook his head at her. ''I only hope your family appreciates the way you protect them.''

She dropped her glance to her lap, embarrassed, and not sure why. ''Just go.''

She didn't hear movement and knew he was hesitating. "Maybe you ought to keep your bedroom door open at night. Just in case."

She eyed him with misgiving. "Just in case what? You get the urge to play Peeping Tom?"

He snorted. "Have it your way. But what if this letter-writing bastard doesn't know your statistics and decides to sneak in your window and do his worst?"

She heard the scrape of his shoe as he turned away. By the time he reached the door, she'd spun around, unable to stop herself. "Okay," she called. "But just a *crack*."

He shifted to glance at her over his shoulder. "That puts a crimp in my Peeping Tom fantasy," he said, "but okay." He flashed a brief grin. The reassuring warmth in it affected Elissa strongly. And that knowledge unsettled her almost as much as the letters.

The Chamber of Commerce Holiday Dinner Dance got off to a rocky start, as far as Elissa was concerned. She hadn't planned to mention it was that night. Unfortunately Jack was also a business owner in Branson, so he'd been invited, too. Much to Elissa's regret, he brought it up, suggesting that it would be a nice change. So Friday evening, December 27, the three couples headed into town in Damien's rental BMW.

Even though Lucy sat up front with Helen and Damien to give those in the back seat more room, Elissa felt as though she's been welded bodily to Alex. Sitting in the middle, she kept peering over at Jack, wondering how such a trim man could take up so much room. Was he doing it on purpose? Poking an elbow in his ribs she asided, "Jack, could you scoot over?"

He grinned at her. "Nope. Sorry."

"You could slide into Alex's lap," Helen suggested.

Elissa glared at the back of her sister's head. Bending forward, she whispered in her ear, "Do you want tomorrow's headlines to read 'Unidentified woman found by roadside'?"

Helen laughed. "You wouldn't do that. My pets need me."

"What are we talking about?" Lucy asked, looking from one sister to the other.

"My pets." Helen met Elissa's gaze in the rearview mirror and she grinned. "And since you're *so* interested, they're all fine. I talked to our house sitter last night. He said the injured owl I rescued is doing much better."

"Your house sitter's that retired veterinarian?" Lucy asked.

"Mmm-hmm. He loves the animals, and of course it makes me feel good to know they're being taken care of properly."

"Injured owl?" Elissa shook her head, almost able to smile about Helen's latest project. She touched Damien's shoulder. "Don't you ever wish she'd give up her hobby of collecting broken creatures?"

Damien laughed. "Don't forget, Lis. I was one of those broken creatures."

Elissa felt a softening at the memory of how Damien had come to their inn. "It seems like forever-ago." She touched Helen's cheek. "Of course, I remember. My baby sister is our little patron saint of—"

"Oh, *please,*" Helen interrupted, sounding self-conscious. "Subject change."

"This is exciting," Lucy chimed in, right on cue. "Jack and I haven't been dancing in a long time. I'm glad you mentioned this, darling." She shifted so that she could better smile at her husband, then eyed Elissa curiously. "I can't believe you forgot, Lis. Usually you're so adamant about attending Chamber functions."

Elissa felt herself flush and hoped the darkness in the car masked her discomfort. "Too much going on, I guess."

"You have been busy," Jack admitted. "Buried in that office of yours. This will do you good."

"Yes, it will." Alex stretched an arm out along the back of the seat, giving them both more room. As his hand brushed her shoulder, she scooted forward until her knees were wedged against the front scat. "You're starting to get coal miner's pallor," he added.

She glared at him. "Thanks. That's the look I was going for."

His grin was teasing and sexy. Hastily she turned away, trying to ignore the hard feel of his leg against her hip. "What were you saying, Lucy?" she asked, desperate to find something else to think about.

Lucy looked puzzled. "Nothing. I just coughed."

"Oh…" Elissa cursed herself for being such a nervous ninny. She'd touched men's thighs before. Alex wasn't poisonous, for heaven's sake.

An eternity passed, her unsettled spirit slightly mollified by the charm of twinkling Christmas decorations they passed as they motored through the snow-covered hills and hollows of the Ozark Mountains. As they entered Branson, a vast animated scene on the mountainside told the story in extravagant shimmering lights that Branson was the home of music, music and more music.

A vote was taken to drive around to view the festival of lights. Elissa tried to get into a festive mood, even though Alex's leg seemed to be pressing harder against her hip. She avoided looking in his direction for fear she would scream, so she looked out of Jack's window.

Lake Taneycomo reflected the holiday lights of Branson's old-fashioned waterfront. Elissa knew any other time she would have been delighted by the festive scenery, but right now all she wanted to do was shove a certain bothersome lawyer into the lake's frosty depths.

"Look up there." Lucy pointed toward the east where Mount Branson displayed its traditional depiction of the Nativity.

"It's even more lovely than I remember," Helen said, her tone hushed.

Along 76 Country Music Boulevard, Elissa felt Alex's arm around her shoulders again, and realized she'd slumped back. Hurriedly she jerked forward. Frantic to give a reason for her abrupt move, she blurted, "Aren't all the theaters beautiful, lit up the way they are! Look there, and there…"

She pointed disjointedly, not caring where she indicated. And it didn't matter. Every building was unique in its own way—from the Andy Williams theater that looked as though it had been carved from the very cliffs, to the Grand Palace, its facade the image of a Southern mansion.

As they drove along the mountain ridge boulevard the whole town gave off a welcoming sparkle. In truth Elissa hardly noticed, her thoughts about Alex D'Amour a conflicting mix of hunger and homicide.

"After the party, let's take a drive down the Trail of Lights," Helen suggested.

"*No!*" Elissa yelled, then cringed at the panic in her voice. "I mean, well—it might be late…"

Jack laughed. "It probably will be."

"Oh, Elissa's right," Lucy admitted. "She does get up early. We should think of her."

"We're here," Damien interjected, as he pulled into

the snow-cleared parking lot to the Lodge of the Ozarks. "Okay, Helen, let's show these folks how to tango."

Helen giggled. "You're so funny."

Jack stepped out of the car, heading around to help his wife out, leaving Alex to assist Elissa. She reluctantly faced her nemesis, giving him an aren't-you-going-to-open-the-door? glare. Withdrawing his arm from around her, he asked, "Do you tango? If you don't I'll teach you."

She chewed on the inside of her cheek, hating having been forced into this untenable position of being Alex's date. But a refusal would have required more explanation than she planned to go into. She glanced toward the front seat. It was empty. The hollow *thud, thud* of doors closing was the only sound in the crisp night. She counted to ten, but it didn't lighten her mood. Meeting Alex's disturbing glance, she muttered, "If my choices were to learn the tango from you, or be devoured in a feeding frenzy of great white sharks, I'd choose the sharks. Is that *perfectly* clear?"

He chuckled and turned to open the door. "Why, Miss Crosby, I had no idea you were such a tease."

The rustic convention center was a Yuletide wonderland of artistic displays of greenery. The ballroom's center-piece was a huge Christmas tree decorated with old-fashioned colored balls, tinsel, ribbons and hand-crafted ornaments.

Alex watched Elissa with wry amusement as she adroitly avoided not only his presence, but every location where mistletoe dangled. He scanned her as she chatted with Yakov Smirnoff, the famous Russian-born comedian who had given an hilarious after-dinner performance. The comedian was laughing at something she said, but they were too far away to hear over the din of conversation and dance music.

Alex slid his glance over her approvingly. Lord, she was gorgeous. Tall and sleek in that long, shapely dress of ivory silk, she gave the impression of being untouchable, like some Grecian column amid an ancient ruin— standing alone and proud, refusing to crumble.

He wasn't a man who mixed business with pleasure, and he knew the knee-happy redhead didn't care much for him, to put it mildly. But being a man who loved a dare, he found her reticence to be on the same planet with him more intriguing than anything he could recall in years. He may have given up his law practice, but he was still damnably aggressive, and he still loved to win. If feisty Miss Elissa Gardenia Crosby wanted him to ignore her, she was going about it the wrong way.

With the cunning intent of a lion stalking a zebra in high grass, Alex made his way toward his prey. A lull in the conversation between the redhead and the comedian presented him with his opening. "It's our dance, Elissa." He nodded toward Yakov. "You put on a great show," he added, meaning it.

Yakov's smile glinted out from his black, curly beard, but before he could respond, he was pulled into a nearby conversation, leaving Alex to draw Elissa into his arms. "Why do I feel like you've been avoiding me?" he asked with a taunting grin.

She went stiff in his arms, and that amused him further.

"Maybe because I *have* been avoiding you," she retorted, her tone as inflexible as her body.

"Ah," he teased. "My instincts are still on target." The music was sensuous and slow. He led her into a turn, adeptly drawing her against him. She was warm, real, not a marble column at all, even though she was making every effort to imitate one.

"If your instincts are so on target, then why are we dancing?"

He chuckled, enjoying the repartee. "You're a challenge, Miss Crosby."

She eyed him with skepticism. "What?" Something seemed to dawn on her, and her green eyes went appealingly wide. "What do you think you're going to do? Seduce me?"

He splayed his hand along the hollow of her back to draw her more firmly against him. "Yes," he whispered.

She sucked in a shocked breath, stiffening again. He quirked a sly grin as he watched her absorb the fact that she had actually relaxed against him. "You have about as much chance at seducing me as you do taking away my inn, buster."

He watched her, saw fear glint in her gaze. She wasn't as sure of herself as she pretended. "Have you heard from your lawyer friend?"

She flinched and he experienced a twinge of compassion. He didn't like putting her out of her home. But it wasn't his fault she'd been duped by a clever con man. These things happened every day. She would come out okay. Elissa Crosby had more backbone than any ten women he knew.

"Dr.—Dr. Grayson's out of his office for a few days. It *is* Christmas vacation, you know. I can't expect him to ignore his family." She lifted her stubborn chin and he fought the urge to kiss it. "He'll have the bad news for you soon enough."

Her voice broke slightly, and his smile faded. She didn't have a leg to stand on, and her vulnerability—one she refused to admit to—got to him.

She watched him with a confused frown, apparently hoping she'd hit a nerve. He supposed she might be thinking he wasn't as sure of himself as she'd thought. That of course wasn't true. He knew exactly how this would turn out. He would own her inn. Period. It was just that the whole matter wasn't quite as black-and-white as it had been two weeks ago—before he'd met her.

A smile snaked across her lips. "What's wrong, Mr. Know-it-all? Afraid?"

He shook off his compassion. This wasn't like him. Annoyed with himself for getting involved in her problems, even for a minute, he forced a cynical grin. "I'm never afraid, Miss Crosby."

As they swayed intimately on the dance floor, he could feel her slim body move subtly against his, her innate sexuality eloquent in its message. He found himself growing more and more aroused by her reluctant nearness, reveling in the womanly feel of her, devouring the beauty of her sparking, jade eyes. Lord, she was a temptress, even when temptation was the last thing on her mind.

Damn the woman! If she would only throw herself at him, he'd grow bored and lose interest. He gazed into those sexy, guarded eyes again, his lips quirking in self-mockery. *Like hell, he would.* Bowing his head, he lowered his face toward hers.

CHAPTER SEVEN

ELISSA sat at the kitchen table, staring at her hands twisted together on the checkered cloth. In her mind's eyes, she didn't see the tablecloth nor her fidgeting fingers. She was witnessing a much more disturbing vision.

She was recalling the dance last night, when she had almost allowed Alex D'Amour to kiss her—*again!* Was she going batty? What had possessed her to lift her chin in invitation? She was angry with herself for her rashness. The romantic lighting, or the soft music, or the gaiety of the party must have made her lower her guard.

Thank heaven, at the last second she'd managed to push him away and march off in a huff—however shaky her legs may have been. His irritating expression lingered in her brain. That sardonic grin. Clearly he'd decided he could come to town, take away her home, her business and—and have his way with *her* as a little bonus!

She had a pretty good idea he didn't think that, now. The only thing she'd said to him since the dance had been a muttered, "How do you carry the weight of your conceit around with you all day?"

She heard a scraping sound and realized she was no longer alone. Helen was opening the back door and the twins, in matching red snowsuits, were scampering outside. Helen didn't have on a coat, so it was obvious she was allowing the girls to go romp in the snow alone.

Alone?

"What are you doing?" Elissa demanded, fear racing

through her. "You're not letting them go out there by themselves, are you?"

Helen looked at her sister with a confused frown. "What?"

Elissa jumped up and dashed to the door to watch the girls. "Never mind. I'll go with them. Run and get my coat from the stairway hall."

Helen started to speak, but Elissa waved her on. "Please! I don't feel good about letting them run around un-unchaperoned." She had almost said unprotected.

Helen shook her head at her sister, then spun to get the coat. From the window in the back door, Elissa watched the twins playing in the snow, squealing with delight. They were so sweet, so dear. She would never forgive herself if anything were to happen to them.

When Helen returned she lay the coat around Elissa's shoulders. "What do you think my babies are going to do, run off and marry the first couple of two-year-old boys they meet?"

Elissa struggled to maintain a calm facade, as she shoved her arms into the coat sleeves. The threatening letters loomed in her mind. On the off chance a nutcase *was* out there, she didn't want her nieces near enough to be harmed. On the other hand, chances were the letter writer was no real threat. Preferring to err on the side of caution, but refusing to worry her sister unnecessarily, she hedged. "It's just that...I've heard there are some...some rabid deer in the area."

"Rabid deer?" Helen echoed, sounding dumbfounded. "I've never heard of rabid deer."

Elissa hadn't, either. *Why had she blurted deer?* Why hadn't she said dogs or at least squirrels? But it was too late now. "Just the same, I'd rather they not go outside alone."

Helen seemed hesitant. "Well, maybe it is better if somebody's with them. Only I have to make some calls to get stuff ready for Damien's birthday party, tomorrow."

"You go make your calls. I'll watch the girls."

Helen squeezed her sister's fingers. "Thanks. It'll only be for fifteen minutes. I told them they could make angels in the snow. That way they'll be good and tired for their naps."

Elissa pulled open the door. "I'll keep an eye on them. Don't worry." Both Jack and Damien had left for New York today—Jack to handle a problem at his New York restaurant, and Damien to do a book-signing. This was no time to start planting worries in Helen's mind about stalkers or threats. She pasted on a teasing grin. "I'm pretty sure no rabid deer will wander by. But better safe than sorry. Right?"

Her sister scanned Elissa's face and seemed mollified by what she saw. She smiled. "Right. So, go make angels in the snow with your nieces."

With a nod, Elissa was out the door like a shot.

She wasn't dressed for making snow angels, so she sat on the back stoop, watching the girls as they romped and squealed and tumbled. A click at Elissa's back told her the door was being opened. "Now, Helen," she said, without turning, "I am perfectly capable—"

"Of avoiding me," Alex finished for her. "I know."

Elissa twisted around to scowl at him, a most unwelcome surprise. Nevertheless, her heart took a foolish leap. "What do you want?"

He held up her boots. "Helen thought you might want these." He scanned her loafered feet, where she'd cleared a spot in the snow for them. "It's a little cold out here for those shoes."

If he were anyone else on earth, she might admit that her toes were grateful for the boots, but since he wasn't anyone else on earth, she turned her back on him.

Much to her regret, in a few seconds, he was sitting on the step beside her. "Here."

The boots thudded into the snow near her feet.

When he said nothing else, she glanced his way. He was watching the twins, his expression somber.

"What's the matter, don't you think they're the most darling girls in the world?" She experienced a rush of petulance. His plan might be to ruin her, but he'd better not find fault with her nieces. That was unthinkable.

He shifted, snagging her gaze. "You're afraid for them, aren't you?" He indicated the twins with a nod. "You think the letter writer might hurt them."

He took up so much space on the stoop, she didn't have a choice but to allow his arm to brush hers. Deciding she didn't need his touch—even coat to coat—she yanked on the snow boots and bolted up. "I'm not afraid, just cautious."

He stood, too. His long lashes made a narrow frame around silver eyes. "You're expecting them to be kidnapped—or worse."

Hiding her fear and her absurd attraction to him, she spat, "Let's just say that by your interference into my life, I've discovered how unpredictable and brutal Fate can be." She waved toward Gilly and Glory. "Those babies are precious to me. If I want to be overprotective, it's *my* business."

"You're a lousy liar, Miss Crosby."

She shot him a deadly look. "Your opinion doesn't interest me, Mr. D'Amour."

A shrill cry rang through the frosty air, and black dread filled Elissa's soul. She scanned the backyard and saw only Gilly. *"Glory!"* she cried, and ran toward the sound as a second cry filled the air.

Rounding the side of the house, Elissa saw her niece stumbling through the snow toward the fence.

"Glory!" she called, catching up to her niece. "Are you okay?" Lifting Glory into her arms, she cried, "What happened?"

Glory's cheeks were pink from exertion and cold, her face animated. She flailed little mittened hands toward the forest.. "Bunny! Bunny! I want bunny!"

"She was chasing a rabbit," Alex said, relief evident in his voice.

Elissa saw tracks in the snow and knew it was true. Inhaling to slow her racing heart, she hugged her niece to her. "Did you see a bunny, sweetie?"

Glory nodded, her cool cheek like velvet against Elissa's jaw. "Can I have bunny, Auntie Lis? Can I?"

Elissa lowered the twin to the snow. "It's a wild bunny, Glory. You wouldn't want to take it away from its family, would you?"

Glory's forehead puckered. "Fam'y?"

Elissa managed a smile. Apparently her niece had never thought of animals as having families. No doubt that was because Helen had rescued so many little creatures, Glory thought all animals wanted to live in houses.

Elissa squatted down so that she was eye level with the toddler. Lovingly she smoothed a dark curl under her red hood. "Now go play. The bunny's gone home."

Glory scampered off to join her sister in a fresh area that needed little snow angels. Elissa watched as she spread her pudgy arms and plopped onto her back in the snow, scooting her legs in and out as she moved her arms up and down.

Weakness invaded Elissa's limbs. She didn't know if

it was relief or delayed reaction to her fear. All she knew for sure was that, all of a sudden, her troubles of the past two weeks had become too much to bear, and a sob issued up from her throat.

Trying to hide her emotions from the ever-vigilant Mr. D'Amour, she spun toward the woods where the rabbit had vanished. Rummaging in her coat pocket for a handkerchief, she managed to swallow a second sob, but couldn't staunch her tears.

She heard Alex's muffled curse and knew he hadn't missed her anguish. Before she could react, he was standing before her, his hand extended, holding a neatly folded handkerchief. "Dammit, Elissa. You have to tell your family. You can't run an inn, worry about being murdered and play watchdog for your nieces. There aren't enough hours in the day. You'll go crazy."

She yanked a wrinkled handkerchief out of her coat pocket, ignoring his overture. "Go *away*." She blew her nose, loudly, even if it wasn't ladylike. Darn him for being there, anyway! Swabbing her eyes, she jammed the handkerchief back into her pocket, feeling more in control. "If you'll recall, you're trying to *steal* my home. If that isn't enough reason to get upset, I don't know what is."

"Dammit, Elissa, I'm not going to throw you out into the snow," he growled. "You can have time to relocate—a month should be sufficient. You simply can't take any reservations after the first of the year."

"And people say you're not a prince!"

"Dammit. I *own* this place. What do you expect—"

"*No!* You're wrong," she interrupted. "You have to be wrong! This inn means everything to me!"

Though his eyes flared, he didn't respond. With a small, frustrated shake of his head, he pivoted away.

Retrieving the hanky from her coat pocket, she dabbed at her eyes, sucking in several deep breaths. The cold air in her lungs felt good. She needed the sting of reality to clear his scent from her nostrils and the clouds of attraction from her brain. She hated the man, for heaven's sake! She hated what he was doing to her and she hated his arrogant attitude that he couldn't be wrong. But worst of all, she hated whatever it was that had gone haywire in her that made him seem—seem so irresistible. And darn the man, he knew how he affected women. He knew he could make her weak for him, even after everything...

Slamming her fists into her pockets, she got hold of herself. She would show him. She was not giving up her inn, and she was not turning away guests. She was not telling her employees they would be out of a job in a few days, and she was not planning to stop taking reservations. Business would go on as usual.

Most importantly of all, she was *not* going to let his charisma affect her. For once in his life, Alex D'Amour, was going to get a rude awakening. He was going to be wrong—about a lot of things!

Fuming, she whirled toward the backyard, but stilled at the sight of the tall, handsome man pulling the giggling girls around on one of the brand-new Christmas sleds that had been leaning against the house. Confounded, she watched him run through the snow to the squealing delight of the twins.

What was his motive? She knew him too well to believe he had any desire to entertain small children. And she would never believe he was doing it as a favor to her. Now that *was* crazy! No, most likely, he was only perpetuating the hoax that they were friends. That had to be it. Helen had come outside onto the small porch and was grinning and waving.

The man was good.

Damien made it back the next day just in time for his birthday party. He and Jack had completed their various projects and made connections at the Springfield airport, riding back together in Damien's rented BMW.

The idea of a party didn't enthuse Elissa. She would have begged off, but she knew she would have seemed terribly antisocial, spending Damien's birthday hiding in her office. Still, Alex's nearness, his heady scent and his speculative gaze—which seemed always to be trained on her—was driving her to distraction.

More than once, that day, she'd experienced a bizarre need to touch him, though she'd resisted. And at breakfast, she'd found herself breathing so deeply of his aroma she'd grown light-headed, almost toppling into his lap. What kind of a fool was she? How could she be attracted to the one man who could take everything she loved away from her?

Though the idea of spending more time in the same room with Alex than absolutely necessary was the last thing Elissa wanted to do, she found the party quite enjoyable. Jule was through for the day as head housekeeper, and had changed into a pretty yellow warm-up. Her husband, Hirk, was there, and had brought little Milhouse. The darling two-year-old played quietly before the fire with the twins. Several of the guests joined in the fun, eating cake and singing "Happy Birthday" to Damien Lord. They were obviously excited to be included in a party for the eminent author and political columnist.

Helen announced they were going to play a game

called "pass the orange," and in a blinding flash the evening turned into Elissa's worst nightmare. She'd never played the game, but she knew it initialed passing the piece of fruit from person to person, without using hands.

Elissa closed her eyes in denial that this was happening, while Helen gathered everyonc into a circle, arranging them boy-girl-boy-girl.

"Okay..." Helen held up a puny orange. "The idea is to pass this around the circle without dropping it. Watch closely."

Elissa clenched her teeth as her younger sister faced Damien, placing the orange between her chin and her collarbone. "Can everybody see? No hands, but you can use just about any other body part to make sure the orange doesn't fall to the floor as you pass it from one person to the next."

With the finesse of an Olympics Orange Passing gold medalist, Damien dipped his chin to Helen's, catching the orange between his jaw and shoulder. A quick tug dislodged the orange from Helen's throat. Now Damien held it jauntily between his chin and chest. Elissa watched with a jaundiced eye. Sure, they made it look easy just to sucker the others into the game, then the naive fools were forced to make jackasses of themselves.

Damien turned to offer the orange to an elderly guest of the inn, placing it between her chin and shoulder.

Elissa took a step backward, deciding this was a good time to escape to her office, but a hand at her elbow halted her. "No, you don't, Miss Crosby."

The hairs on her nape stood up and she peered sideways. "Where did you come from?"

"California," Alex said with a grin.

She tugged on his hold, but not very hard. She didn't

want to draw attention to the fact that she had an aversion to having Alex's jaw close enough to hers to kiss, er, touch! "That's just *so* amusing," she asided in a surly whisper.

He indicated the game. "It's almost your turn."

"I'm not playing."

He lifted a brow. "Chicken, Miss Crosby?"

She knew he was baiting her but she didn't care. "I don't like games played with fruit."

He chuckled. "There are a few I could teach you that I bet you'd like."

She inhaled a scandalized breath. What was he talking about? Kinky sex? She backed away, but found her exit thwarted by his hold at her elbow.

"Elissa," Helen called. "Poor Hirk is getting a stiff neck. It's your turn."

She jumped at the sound of her name and turned around. At least, she turned as far as she could with Mr. Oh-No-You-Don't still clutching her. With a fake grin and a frosty rebuke in her eyes, she shifted back to face Alex. "I need my arm."

His bow as he let her go was almost imperceptible. She felt the urge to run, but knew it was too late. Hirk was waiting with an orange stuck in his neck. With a smile of apology to everyone for holding up the game, she faced Hirk. "Okay, Boggs, let's do it."

The tall, gangly man bent to present her with the orange. Being a shy person, he made every effort to insert the fruit between Elissa's jaw and collarbone without any embarrassing touching. She liked that about Hirk. Shy and polite. Unlike some people—arrogant and rude—standing on the *other* side of her.

Once the orange was secure, she stiffly turned to deposit it against Alex's throat. Her intent was to get rid of it and away from him with great dispatch. When their eyes met, he grinned, and a shudder of apprehension went through her. Why did she have the feeling his plans didn't coincide with hers? "Don't do anything stupid," she whispered.

"I never do anything stupid," he breathed into her ear as he leaned down to receive her orange.

At first the transfer seemed to be going fine. However, a millisecond after Elissa released the orange, Alex said, "Whoops."

"Whoops?" she echoed, unable to catch the orange against her jaw. The darned thing had rolled too far down her chest. Still, it didn't drop. Alex had saved it with his cheek, and now was rolling it along her sweater.

"Sorry." His gaze lifting to meet hers, his eyes alight with mischief. "I'll get it. Don't worry."

Hating the need to do it, she thrust her chest out to help him coax the orange toward his jaw. With excruciating slowness, he maneuvered the fruit from the rise of one breast clear across the other.

His cheek brushed her breasts, then his chin, then his shoulder, as he twisted and turned to move the orange. By that time, it had made the trip across her body, Elissa and Alex were pressed together chest to breast. Their arms wide while they rubbed and bumped against each other in the struggle to get the wayward orange into the hollow of Alex's throat. At least *she* was struggling toward that goal.

"I'm about to get it. One more second," he said, his eyes dancing with fun.

She harbored strong reservations about Alex's assurances. The orange slid up a bit, but not enough for her to catch it with her chin. Darn Alex D'Amour! She knew he was doing this on purpose, just to make her miserable.

He rolled the orange up slightly, inching it toward her shoulder. She had a flash of hope that she was seconds away from snagging it with her jaw. Her breasts were pressed hard against his chest as he continued to nudge the fruit with his shoulder to a fraction of an inch below her collarbone. *Just a little further!* she pleaded inwardly.

Trying desperately to concentrate on the game, and ignore the tormenting hardness of his body, she dipped slightly, curving her shoulder forward in an effort to trap the orange. Alex lifted his glance to hers and she froze. Their lips were so close. So close...

His breath was warm and tempting against her mouth, and she felt a tremor of desire. She knew how those lips felt, how they made her feel. Though she'd promised herself never to touch them again, the sexy rat was making the vow difficult to keep.

"Just one more second," Alex said, loud enough for everyone to hear.

"Oh, no, hurry," Jack called through a laugh.

"Good game," Damien said. "Next time let's do it with a pea."

Another burst of laughter filled the room. Alex's scent was everywhere—in her nostrils, her brain. She was woozy. Those irritating silver eyes beckoned. Her pulse was reaching levels that went far beyond merely disloyal. As Alex moved against her in a grueling, meandering trek to relocate the dratted orange, their hips and bellies stroked and bumped, sometimes locking together for long seconds filled with sweet torture. The masculine texture of his body taunted and aroused, making her weak. If she didn't act quickly, she would actually be kissing the man in front of God and everybody.

Desperate to be free of his spell, she took an abrupt

step backward, allowing the orange to fall to the oriental rug with a soft *thud*.

"Oh dear," she said, feigning distress.

"Elissa!" Laughing, Helen headed through the circle toward her. "I hope you know what you've done."

Elissa shook out her curls, breathing deeply to regain her poise. "I'm sorry. I guess that means I'm out?"

"Don't you know how the game goes?" Helen retrieved the orange. "Now you have to kiss Alex."

"Really?" Alex flashed a crooked grin. "Elissa. You flirt."

How could she have forgotten such a terrifying rule? She sensed that her face had gone as red as her hair, and she feared her head would explode from fury. How dare Alex tease her! After all, he was the cause of her dropping the darned orange.

Ignoring her pledge to keep her animosity for Alex a secret, she opened her mouth to tell him what she thought of him, and to inform him of exactly what hot place she hoped he would go.

Before she could shout out a single syllable, Alex took her face in his hands and kissed her. Hard. His lips held such sizzling persuasion that she forgot that she was going to shout at him. She forgot the other people in the room. She forgot her name. And she forgot that the man making her toes tingle with his kiss was her worst enemy.

Elissa tossed off her blankets, moaning. She couldn't sleep, angry with herself for allowing a ruthless landgrabber any power over her heart. Half the night she'd tossed and turned, trying not to think about his disturbing kiss.

Her memory of it was blurred and foggy, which was unlike her. She could only vaguely remember babbling about needing to get some bills paid, then skittering down the stairs to hide in her office. She'd gotten little accomplished, except for trembling and blinking back tears, and she hardly called that an achievement.

She refused to think about her feelings. She'd always seen herself as an independent person, completely self-reliant. Alex D'Amour was her enemy. Did he think his expertise in seduction would make her surrender her efforts to keep her inn? Well, if that was his plan, it wouldn't work. Dr. Grayson would be back in his office tomorrow, and she would be able to talk with him, find out how he and his staff were progressing with her ownership problem. Very soon she would have the bothersome Mr. D'Amour out of her heart, er, *hair!*

Scrambling from her bed she slid into her Goofy slippers and grabbed her robe. Knotting the sash, she shoved the vision of a pair of beguiling eyes to a back shelf of her brain.

And that kiss!

The wild, wondrous taste of his lips loomed in her mind, making her stumble, and she sagged against the wall to get her equilibrium back. She couldn't allow the thought of that kiss to keep creeping into her consciousness. She had to get some sleep. Warm milk might help. She'd heard it settled the nerves. The way things stood, she'd probably have to heat about twelve gallons, but she might as well try it. She wasn't getting any rest, anyway.

Quietly she pulled open the door and tiptoed past the unfolded sofa, averting her glance. She had no desire to look at Alex. And even if she had, it was so dark she could barely find her way to the stairs, let alone make out a reclining figure in the rumpled covers.

She scurried up the steps and rounded the corner into

the kitchen before she realized the light was on. Coming to a skidding halt, she was overcome with distress to see Alex sitting at the kitchen table, a mug of steaming coffee in his hand. He glanced up, his long lashes casting a shadow across his eyes. The harsh, overhead light made his solemn features seem carved from stone. She had a feeling he'd been thinking very dark thoughts and she wondered what they might be. "Troubles?" she asked, daring to hope he was doubting his ownership of her inn.

He set down his mug and stood, startling her with the gentlemanly move. He was wearing a blue cashmere sweater and jeans. His hair was tousled, and he looked charmingly unkempt, as though he hadn't been able to sleep, either. His lips curved at one corner as he scanned her attire, from her bulky terry robe to her comical slippers. "What's this? A late-night rendezvous with a lover?"

She tugged her lapels together, feeling naked under his scrutiny. "That's right, avoid answering the question by taking the offensive."

"I didn't' realize I was being offensive."

She sniffed, shuffling around him to retrieve a pan for her milk. "You're always offensive, Mr. D'Amour. Maybe you should have that fact tattooed on the back of your hand as a quick reference."

His chuckle rumbled through her, though he was a good three feet away. "What are you doing?"

"Heating milk, if it's any of your business."

"Why?"

She shifted around, eyeing him with more affront than she felt. His nearness was wreaking havoc on her insides. "To make it *hot*."

He grinned outright then. "Why don't you just kiss it?"

The not-so-subtle reminder set her blood on fire, but she masked it by bristling. "Don't be crude!"

"I thought I was complimenting you." Though he was still grinning, the expression was less teasing this time. More contemplative. "I've been sitting here thinking about your kiss—and how good it might be if you let yourself enjoy it." The challenge that lit his gaze made her legs go wobbly. "It's a hell of a thought."

She stared at him, speechless. What was he saying? Had he been as affected by their kiss as she? Realizing her lips had dropped open, she clamped her jaws shut, shaking off the notion. He was playing with her again. Darn the man and his talent for playacting. She was not one of his half-witted conquests who would come softly into his arms, giving him anything he wanted. "That's something you'll never know, Mr. D'Amour." She cleared an odd raspiness from her throat.

He shrugged those sinfully wide shoulders, so casual and elegant, she wanted to scream. He could sure turn it off as quickly as he could turn it on. "Having trouble sleeping?" he asked.

She spun away to get the milk out of the refrigerator. Why was it that he could make her furious by merely existing, but she couldn't seem to rattle him with direct insults? When she turned back, she scowled. "No, I'm not having trouble sleeping. I'm always up for the three o'clock milk warming ceremony."

He lounged against the table, his expression serious. "You didn't get another threatening letter, did you?"

"No." She turned her back and poured milk into the pan. Her hand shook, but by some miracle she managed not to spill it. "I don't care to discuss it." She switched on the gas and returned the carton to the refrigerator before she faced him again.

He was watching her, arms crossed. "Then what's wrong? Did you hear from your lawyer friend?"

She rummaged in a shelf to get a mug, refusing to answer.

"I gather you didn't. At least not good news."

"I *will*," she warned, brandishing the mug.

His gaze shifted to the stovetop, then back to her face. "What are you burning?"

She peered at the milk. It wasn't even steaming yet. "I know how to warm milk and it's not burning." She turned away. "Drink your coffee and leave me alone."

He was silent for a minute, and Elissa could feel his stare. She knew her shoulders were too rigid, but she couldn't even pretend to be relaxed under his watchful gaze. Why didn't he go away?

"Something really is burning, Elissa."

The urgency in his tone made her jerk around. When she did, he was running out of the kitchen, toward the front of the house.

Suddenly she could smell it, too.

"*Oh, Lord!*" she cried, her mug crashing to the floor. "*My inn's on fire!*"

on the and remained the outside. Preke felt an a better audience that figures.

He was welcome to — this evening? Then what a though It would hear from what hower chose.

She welcomed the figure turning meaning, helping to make

CHAPTER EIGHT

THE fire apparently started when one of the Christmas lights around the outside of the parlor window had shorted out, igniting nearby decorative greenery. Alex's quick thinking made fast work of putting out the blaze. But just to be safe, Elissa roused the guests and hustled them outdoors. They huddled in their cars, wrapped in blankets, until the fire marshal determined it was safe to go back in.

Luckily the damage was mainly relegated to the outside front wall of the parlor where paint was blistered and wood, charred. The parlor window had broken from the heat, and the curtains were ruined, but thankfully no one had been hurt and the damage inside had been minimal.

The guests were shaken by the experience, but they were reassured that their rooms were safe. There hadn't even been smoke damage on the second floor. When Bella arrived, she promised a special breakfast, to take everyone's minds off the fire.

After the guests were safely back in their rooms, Elissa ran downstairs to change into trousers and a bulky sweater. When she dashed toward the front door to help in the cleanup, Alex grabbed her arm. "This was no accident, Elissa." His expression was grim as he herded her away from her brothers-in-law, coming inside after nailing plywood over the broken window. "Dammit, woman, don't you think it's time you told your family what's been going on?"

From the reception hall, Elissa cast a peek at Damien and Jack as they prepared to tape plastic over the inside of the broken window. Sucking in a determined breath, she faced Alex. His cheek was streaked with soot, as were his forearms, where he'd rolled up his sweater. He looked dear, and she fought a softening for him. It was true he'd done her a good deed, but she had no intention of allowing him to make more trouble for her. "Of course it was an accident," she whispered. "The fire marshall determined the cause as a short in the wiring."

"The fire marshall doesn't know what we know."

"It was an *accident,* Alex." Elissa pulled from his grip. "Stop acting like Chicken Little, with your shouting, 'The sky is falling...the sky is falling!'"

"Why don't you pull your head out of the sand, Miss Ostrich?"

She slanted another glance at her brothers-in-law. They were busy with the repair and clearly didn't notice a fight going on. With a withering glare at Alex, she spat, "You're being paranoid."

"You're be naive." His eyes were narrow, flashing slits.

How dare he be so disagreeable and hardheaded! "I hate stubborn, argumentative people!" she retorted.

"Oh, sweetheart..." His chuckle was bitter. "You, of all people, don't want to go there."

She could recognize sarcasm when she heard it, and she didn't give a fig if he thought she was hardheaded and stubborn. With a toss of her head, she resolved to move the subject back on track. "I refuse to upset my sisters with useless worry."

"Upset them?" he repeated, cynically. "They were rousted out of bed in the middle of the night, forced to huddle in the freezing cold for two hours. It's just a guess, but I'd say they're already upset."

"Well, I don't intend to upset them further," she said, under her breath. "Anyway, how could it be arson?"

He exhaled, sounding exasperated. "It doesn't take that much brains to know how to make a string of Christmas lights short out. A kid could do it."

A tremor rushed through her. "You're too suspicious," she charged, denying the ugly idea with all her being. "Don't invent crimes where none exist."

He stared at her, the incredulity in his gaze mutating into suspicion. "Please tell me you didn't do this, yourself—as some sort of empty act of defiance against me. I'm razing the place for the golf course, anyway. Burning it down would only make my work easier."

She gasped, horrified by the very suggestion. "How could you—" Her voice broke, and she struggled to control herself. "How could you believe such a thing for one second? Everything—*everybody*—I love is in this inn!" She glared at him. Revulsion in her tone, she demanded, "Have you ever loved anybody, Alex? It's not possible, or you couldn't suggest such a hideous thing!"

His nostrils flared. "I know all about love, Miss Crosby. Oh, yes. I had the best teachers. My parents were totally devoted to each other. That's why they shipped me off to boarding school, so I wouldn't interfere with their 'great love.'" He spat the last two words out contemptuously.

"Would you like to know how I spent my holidays every year?" he challenged. "With five or six other boys who'd also been discarded by self-serving parents. The headmaster would take us skiing once or twice between Christmas and New Year's. The rest of the holidays, we spent in regimented tedium, with plenty of time on our hands to dwell on the fact that all we had in our meager, lonely lives—was money." His eyes flashed with emotion. "As far as I'm concerned, love is synonymous with selfishness. So don't talk to me about love. I've had a bellyful."

The hurt in his voice, his shimmering gaze, was so staggering, it reached out, ripping through the wall of her anger, and grabbed her by the heart, causing pain. Barely aware of her actions, she took his hands. "Oh—oh, Alex…"

There was a change in his expression, something almost expectant lit his eyes, making her realize what she'd done. Stunned by her rashness, she yanked her hands away. This lonely-little-boy story was probably a well-rehearsed part of his plan to wear her down. Since seduction hadn't worked, he'd decided to try pity. Animosity tightened her gut. "If selfishness is the same thing as love to you, Mr. D'Amour," she cried, "then you're a very *loving* man!"

Spinning on her heel, she marched into the parlor as Jack gave the last piece of duct tape a final swipe of his hand. "That should take care of it until we can get it repaired," he was saying.

She headed toward her brothers-in-law, hoping Alex would get the hint and go away. Damien was taking down the ladder when Elissa stopped him and gave him a hug. "Thanks." Turning to Jack, she kissed his cheek. "You, too." Backing away she smiled tiredly. "Now both of you get to bed. Lucy and Helen should have the twins down by now."

Jack slung an arm around her shoulders. "You're taking this pretty well." He squeezed her affectionately. "But then, what would I expect from Mother Elissa."

A lump formed in her throat. She cared deeply for

both Jack and Damien. It was funny, but her maternal inclination toward her sisters extended to their husbands now. It was irrational, she knew. Both men were well equipped to care for their own families. But she'd mothered her sisters for so many years, she wasn't quite able to relinquish the parental role she'd become accustomed to playing. Besides, she'd decided long ago it was her lot in life to take on the burdens, in order to spare those she loved from pain.

Alex's suggestion about arson nagged at her, forcing alarming visions to crowd her mind. Surely nobody had set that fire on purpose. Surely it was exactly what the fire marshal said. An accident. And her fault, for forgetting to turn off the lights. That was all. Human error combined with an old string of lights. Nobody could want to hurt her family; it was too horrible a thought to even imagine.

Though unable to trust her voice, she managed to hold on to her brave smile. Squeezing Jack's hand, she murmured, "All's well that ends well. Now, you two go on to bed." It came out a little husky.

Jack and Damien gathered up the rest of the unused plastic, duct tape and ladder, and were quickly gone. With an exhausted exhale, she allowed her shoulders to slump. Switching off the parlor lights, she dragged herself to the leather chair that sat beside the hearth. Glowing embers were the room's only illumination, and darkness suited her mood. Sagging into the chair, she stared into the shadows, her fists clenched. The stench of burned wood and fabric stung her nostrils, the eerie quiet somehow frightening.

She felt numb, brain-dead. Thoughts wouldn't track to a logical conclusion. They became confused, muddled, butting up against spikes of panic, then ricocheted around her head like terrified mice, running for their lives and finding no refuge.

"Maybe I am insolent and unfeeling, Elissa," came Alex's familiar voice, "but I was forced to become that way because all I had to count on was myself. What's your excuse for being so detached?" She heard his muffled footfalls cross the rug. "You have a family you refuse to confide in. They love you. Why don't you let them help?" He stopped, not far away. "Do you know how many people would give *anything* for—" He cut himself off, but in those few words Elissa learned a great deal.

Alex envied her close family. Envied! She could see it now—the poor little rich kid, shipped off to fancy boarding schools, full of strict rules and regimens, by selfish, jet-set parents. He may have taken ski trips to Colorado every holiday, but they hadn't made up for the warmth of a loving family, laughing and joking before a holiday fire. No wonder he knew nothing about opening gifts at dawn, or Christmas dinners served in the middle of the afternoon, timetables be damned. He had grown up a child of regulations and timetables. He'd had to claw a place for himself in the world—all alone.

With gritted teeth, she shoved the realization back. Didn't she have enough trouble without taking on the childhood hurts of her worst enemy?

She shifted to glower at him. "You could have set the fire—to force us out." The accusation was empty— nothing more than an attempt to divert attention from a discussion of her relationship with her family. Still, her anguish spurred her to go on. "Like you said, you're going to tear the place down, anyway."

He blinked, clearly thunderstruck, but before he could respond, she held up a halting hand, "Okay, okay, I don't believe you did it.'' She turned away, muttering determinedly, ''It was an *accident*.'' After a long, silent moment, she rose, terribly weary. ''This isn't your concern, Alex,'' she whispered. ''I can handle it.''

''Before or after something happens to those little girls?'' he demanded. ''Is your self-reliance that important to you?''

The indictment cut deep and she bled from her soul. He'd hit on a painful truth. Lifting her gaze to meet his, she fought tears. ''My self-reliance has gotten me and my sisters through some tough times—those years after Mom died, and then when Jack's mother paid no attention to us. Daddy had to be gone a lot. He worked hard. Somebody had to take charge, be the mother. Somebody had to—''

''Lucy and Helen are all grown up.'' He took her by the arms, giving her a shake. ''Dammit, Elissa, you have one hell of a family, fully capable of helping you. You keep yourself so separated from them, and they don't even realize it, do they?''

A tear slid down her cheek, and she shook her head denying his accusation, scarcely aware of the irony that she was answering his question. Yet, another irony did strike her, and that was how only Alex D'Amour, so emotionally isolated all his life, could see the truth. Maybe it took one to know one.

Witnessing her tears seemed to do something to Alex's anger, and his features grew less harsh. ''Do you have any idea who the pervert is that's doing this?'' he asked more gently. ''An old law client, maybe?''

She inhaled a shuddery breath, trying to regain herself. ''Get off it! Nobody did this!''

With a mumbled curse, he tugged her into his embrace, but she was too emotionally fragile to fight him.

Nuzzling the crook of his neck, she inhaled. Even mixed with the acrid smell of smoke, his scent made her heart grow lighter. Without analyzing why, she allowed her arms to snake around his back as he held her. His jaw was rough against her cheek, and for some crazy reason that made her feel better, too. Her fingers spread, relishing the feel of cashmere over supple muscle. The combination was heady, stirring, and she found herself leaning greedily into him, delighting in the feel of his powerful body—so big and sheltering. Oh, to be protected. It was a luxury she'd never allowed herself. But sometimes, deep in the night, there were moments when she longed for...

"Elissa, you have to tell your family." His warm breath ruffled her hair. "If you don't, I will."

Reality intruded with his quiet threat and she went ramrod stiff, drawing away. She could tell he meant what he said, and a shaft of panic stabbed her. She had to prevent him from doing that—somehow.

"Don't you dare!"

His eyes drilled into hers. There was nothing in his expression that told her he planned to give her any more leeway in the matter.

Flailing for any straw to hold onto, she pleaded, "What if I report the fire to the police? Let them decide." Lifting a determined chin, she added, "The fire marshall said some kids had been setting fires around town. Even if it were arson, it was probably a prank. Kids. Promise me you won't bother my family with unfounded suspicions." She reached out to take his arms in a beseeching gesture, then thought better of touching him. "Please, Alex?" She balled her fists. "Can't you understand, you're overreacting."

His brows dipped, and she could see deep disapproval in his expression.

She wrung her hands. *"Please?"*

His continued silence made her want to scream. At her wits end, she promised, "I'll take in what's left of the string of lights. They can have it checked out. If they find anything suspicious…" She shrugged again. "Then, of course I'll let my family know.

He watched her for an endless moment, his gaze searching. Finally he nodded. "Report it. Take in the lights. I doubt if there's enough left to tell much, but at least they'll know."

"Promise you won't say anything to my family."

When Alex opened his mouth to speak, she gave him a look that was meant to be murderous, but she feared all she could muster was despair.

"Hell…" Reluctance hardened his tone. "Okay, I won't say anything—yet. But I think you're wrong to put it off."

"You know what I think of your opinion," she said, trying to regain the emotional distance she needed.

His expression harsh, he looked away. Elissa watched with grim fascination as he battled to keep his temper. When he snagged her gaze again, he shook his head. "Dammit, Elissa, you're one tough woman. Sometimes I want to strangle you and sometimes—" He stopped, the cynical quirk of his lips telegraphing frustration. "Forget it. You don't give a damn about my opinion."

"You're learning." She was lying when she said his opinion didn't mean anything to her. He'd called her tough, and suddenly she *was* tough—stronger, somehow. It was an odd reaction to a few grumbled words, but right now she'd take anything she could get.

Feeling more capable than she had in days, she made a haughty exit, heading off to get herself a cup of coffee.

"When are you going to town?" he asked.

She closed her eyes, counting to ten. "As soon as I have breakfast—*mother*."

"Would you like me to go with you?"

She spun around, her glower locking with his in open warfare. "Do I *look* like I want you to go?"

His crooked grin told her he'd received her go-to-hell message. "On second thought…" He lifted his hands in a resigned gesture, and took a step backward. "I think I'll just gather up what's left of that string of lights and put it in your car for you."

Elissa was back from Branson before the rest of her family was up and around. She breathed a sigh of relief about that. Though the officer she spoke with seemed receptive, he didn't leap over his desk and force her into protective custody. He had taken her report and the lights, acted attentive and said it would be looked into.

She was thankful everybody wasn't as much of an alarmist as Alex. He'd almost had her believing the arson foolishness for a while. Well, she'd held up her end of the bargain and told the police. They'd admitted making no headway with the letters, and at least a dozen of her old clients hadn't been located, yet. So the case was still wide-open. Any one of them could be lurking in the area. With hundreds of tourists coming and going every day, finding the letter-writer among them—without any further leads than they had—was close to impossible.

As for the string of lights—thousands of fires were caused by defective Christmas lights every year. From the look she saw in the sergeant's eyes, she was sure he felt this was another accident. Oh, he would follow up and do whatever had to be done, but she doubted if it would give them any clues. So, basically, nothing had changed. It was still a waiting game.

Snow began to fall at ten o'clock that morning, a peaceful sight. Elissa only wished her emotions were up to enjoying the beauty of the winter wonderland. Unfortunately too many problems were preying on her mind to give her room for serene contemplation of the miracle of a snowflake.

The continued frigid temperature kept work from being done on Alex's mansion, which had no heat due to reconstruction. That shouldn't be her problem, but it was. For it meant that he would remain underfoot at the inn. *All day long.*

On the plus side, the last guest had checked out, everyone going home for New Year's Eve. This was the first time since Elissa had opened the inn that she had no guests on New Years. She had to admit, if only to herself, that she was grateful. This year she needed to be able to enjoy the celebration with her family, unencumbered by the needs of strangers. Of course, Alex D'Amour would be there—unless she received happy news from Dr. Grayson, tomorrow. She crossed her fingers that she would.

At one o'clock, she retired to her room for a power nap and slept for two hours. Stretching, she got up, refreshed. She attempted to reach Dr. Grayson, but could do no more than leave a message on his voice mail.

She tried to read good news into the fact that he was out—and that he hadn't called her back. She couldn't. Yet, she couldn't read bad news into it, either. Thinking about it would only drive her crazy. She forced it from her mind, telling herself that her fate couldn't be in more capable hands than Dr. Grayson's.

On her way upstairs, she heard Helen call her name.

"What?" she asked, bounding to the top step.

"You're up at last. We've been waiting."

Rounding the corner into the kitchen, she saw Helen, Damien and Alex sitting around the table, steamy cups of coffee in their hands. She could smell dinner in the oven—a roast Bella had put on to cook before she'd left for the day.

Damien smiled at Elissa. "You look rested." He scanned her, a wave of dark hair slipping down over his forehead. He was such a handsome man, and so dear, she didn't even notice his scars any longer. When his glance met hers again, he said, "Run back down to your room and put on jeans. We're going sledding."

"We are?" Foreboding slithered along Elissa's spine. She hoped by "we" they meant she, Helen and Damien, but she had a feeling Alex's presence was a bad sign.

"It's so lovely out." Helen flung an arm toward the window. "With the snow coming down and all. It's perfect."

Elissa's glance skittered to Alex, who was watching her, his lips lifted sensuously at each corner. The expression was not so much one of amusement, but more an inquiry. He knew how badly she wanted to avoid his company, and watching her attempt to squirm out of it seemed to intrigue him.

"Now, hurry." Helen made shooing motions. "We've waited an hour for you, already."

"You shouldn't have bothered," Elissa mumbled, her brain going foggy. Why couldn't she come up with any excuse not to go? She was usually pretty quick-witted in situations like this.

She was at a disadvantage, though, since they already knew the place had no guests and that she'd taken a nap.

They knew if she said no it would be because she didn't want to spend time with them. And that wasn't true. She'd love to go, if it were only Helen and Damien.

A thought sprang to her mind. "What about the twins?"

"Lucy and Jack are going to baby-sit," Helen said, taking a sip of her coffee.

Elissa cringed inwardly. Of course. In Lucy's condition, she wouldn't want to go speeding down bumpy hills on a sled. "Oh…"

"You need to get out and have a little fun," Alex coaxed, and she had a feeling he meant it.

There was a great deal of truth to his statement. It would ease her nerves to get some exercise. She glanced out the kitchen window. The woods beyond the house were picture-perfect, with big flakes fluttering down all around. It looked like a Christmas card. Elissa faced the fact that she desperately needed to loosen up—have some fun—or she would explode into a million schizoid pieces.

With a decisive nod, she hurried down the stairs and changed into sledding clothes.

It turned out to be a good thing Alex came along, since the best sledding hill was on his property. Elissa was having a great time, even though Damien and Helen shared one sled and Alex and she shared the other. She'd insisted on taking turns with him, sliding down one at a time, even though Helen and Damien doubled up.

Elissa trudged back up the hill after her turn to find Alex standing alone at the crest of the hill. He lounged against an ancient oak.

"Hi." He lifted a gloved hand in a casual salute.

"Hi, yourself." She grinned, feeling too good to growl. Sledding had been exactly what she'd needed.

She felt wholly alive for the first time in ages. Turning toward the slope, she scanned the nearby wood. Between the uppermost branches, she could make out two of the chimneys of the D'Amour mansion. Off to her left she could see the peaked roof of her Victorian inn. "It's nice here," she murmured. "I've never walked this far onto your property in the winter before."

He didn't respond, so she turned. He was idling there, his arms loosely folded across his chest as he watched her. His gaze was so intense, she lost her smile. Feeling embarrassed, and not sure why, she turned away.

"How'd it go with the police?" he asked.

She grew rigid, refusing to face him. "I imagine by now they're firmly convinced that I'm an hysterical female—seeing bogeymen behind every tree." She peered at him. "Thanks to you."

"I should have gone with you."

"No you shouldn't," she retorted. "I don't need a man's validation. As far as the letters go, the investigation is ongoing." She averted her gaze. "Could we talk about something else? We've wasted enough time on your desperado theory."

"Look, Elissa—"

"Where are Damien and Helen?" she interrupted, yanking her knit cap further down over her ears.

"Okay, okay," he said. "If that's the way you want it. Damien and Helen headed off down the other side."

Glancing around, she noticed the sled tracks. "Oh?" She retrieved the pull rope on her sled. "Good idea. Maybe it's time to find another hill."

She tromped in the direction of the tracks, but as she passed Alex, he grasped the rope, halting her progress. "I wouldn't if I were you."

She peered at him, confused.

"I think they're—" he lifted a meaningful brow "—busy."

Her bewilderment vanished at his explicit tone. Visions of Damien and Helen, making wild love somewhere beyond the line of trees, sprang into her mind. "Oh, that's crazy. They wouldn't go off and..." The sentence trailed away. The idea of discussing sex with this man disturbed her.

He shrugged, his eyes twinkling. "I've heard it happens."

Elissa sensed that Alex was right, and she could feel her cheeks go hot. Helen and Damien were so in love she might as well accept the obvious. They were melting snow somewhere in the woods, making impetuous love. She didn't realize she'd let her gaze drop until she felt a tug on the rope to regain her attention. "I have a feeling you're going to have a lot of nieces and nephews."

When she met his gaze again, she was struck by what she saw. His eyes were glinting with pure, masculine interest. Suddenly, out there in the cold beauty of an Ozark winter, she became overwhelmingly aware of his rugged, manly appeal. He wore no hat, and glittering snow spangled his dark hair. His long legs, all sinewy muscle, were crossed at the ankle, and seemed to go on and on.

For so long, her attention had been focused on her inn, why did her repressed libido have to come to life now? She feared if she didn't watch her step, she and Alex D'Amour would do a little snow melting of their own.

No! her mind screamed, as she tried to get back on track. Sucking in a frigid breath of air, she tugged the rope from his hands. "I'm—I'm tired of sledding. Let's go back."

"Okay."

His capitulation was so offhand she grew suspicious and scanned his face to gauge his expression. He looked perfectly at ease. Why she'd expected an argument she didn't know.

"But since the inn's downhill, we might as well go by sled."

We? There was that dastardly word, again. Now she understood why he'd been so contented with the idea. She faced him, thrusting the sled's rope at him. "I'll walk back. You can sled."

He didn't reach for it, but merely smiled. "What are you afraid of, Miss Crosby? It's a sled, not a motel room."

She swallowed, going wooden. Her arm remained stuck out toward him. She couldn't seem to move, and wondered if some evil forest spirit had turned her into a hitching post.

He took the rope from her fingers. "You get down on the sled and I'll lie on top of you."

When his suggestion soaked in, she did a double-take. "An alien spaceship will beam me up before *that* happens."

He chuckled. "Or, you can be on top."

Her face was flaming. Even with an IQ of a table lamp, nobody could miss the sexual innuendo in that remark. She planted her hands on her hips, eyeing him with disdain. Unfortunately some unruly beast inside her was giving her fits, trying to get her mouth to say "yes." She struggled with it, valiantly forming a biting, negative response that under no circumstances could be mistaken for, "Okay…"

She frowned, looking around. *Who said that?*

Before she could deal with the shocking fact that she

had agreed to his plan, he was lying prone on the sled. Rising up on one elbow, he asked, "Ready?"

She glared at him, not believing what was happening. But even as she took a step away from him, that same vile, incorrigible, disobedient wanton beast inside her forced her next step to be forward—toward him and his waiting back. As if by magic, she found herself standing over him.

"Okay, I'm braced," he said with a grin.

She gave him an impatient smirk. "I don't weigh *that* much."

He laughed. "I know. I thought you might jump on me with both feet."

Her smirk was hijacked by the incorrigible beast inside her, and she found herself smiling. "Don't give me any ideas."

With a playful wag of his brows, he cocked his head. "Come on, I'm getting cold."

She scrambled to straddle him, muttering, "That'll be the day."

Once she was lying on his back, she grabbed his shoulders and shouted, "Go!" Her objective was to get this thing over before she completely lost her mind.

He pushed off and they headed down the long incline. The race through cold air and fluttering snow was exhilarating, but not nearly as thrilling as the feel of his taut hips against her thighs. She could detect every flex of muscle in his shoulders and his legs, registering the sensations with heart-pounding single-mindedness. He maneuvered around a curve in the hill, and she squealed, burying her head in his neck. She sucked in a breath of him, enjoying the experience much more than she should.

As she lifted her face again, he steered the sled

sharply left, barely missing a little cedar. "Are you trying to kill us?" she shrieked, laughing.

"I hate back seat drivers," he shouted.

"I'm not crazy about you, either!" She squealed as they took another turn. The beast inside her made her burst out with a delighted peal of laughter. Then it forced her to her curl her feet around his legs, clamping her body even tighter against his. *Darn beast!*

His next turn was even sharper, and they skidded sideways for what seemed to be an eternity before gravity won out and they spilled into soft snow. As she was thrown off his back, she instinctively grabbed his shoulders. When they came to rest, she found herself sprawled beneath him.

As the laughter stopped, their eyes met.

Alex brushed snow from her cheek, whispering, "Fantasies do come true."

She lay there, looking into his remarkable face, his body, hot and hard, blanketing hers. His soft smile, those exotic eyes mesmerized her.

"You did that on purpose," she accused softly, unable to conjure up a shred of real indignity.

His answer was the hunger she could see in his eyes, as he lowered his lips to hers.

CHAPTER NINE

ELISSA found herself surrendering to the wonder of his kiss. Her senses filled with his texture and scent, and she kissed him back with all the passion she possessed. Breathless and with urgent abandon, she wrapped her arms around him, her embrace as wild and hungry as her kiss.

He moaned against her lips, clearly aware of the change in her attitude. His mouth moved over hers, his hot kiss becoming a provocative request. The fires inside her shot upward and outward, and with a surge of joy, she opened her lips inviting him to fully possess her mouth.

With a sensuous rhythm, his tongue joined hers in a soundless, writhing dance. Caressing, thrusting with increased urgency, his tongue sent her spiraling toward new heights of sensation. Sizzling desire roared through her, feelings that were both alien and exquisite. No other man had ever affected her this way, making her bold, unafraid—even eager—to share herself fully.

As his kisses grew white-hot, his body began to move suggestively against hers. Though some faint voice in her brain shrieked that this man was her enemy, that she was a fool to let this happen, she couldn't bring herself to pull away.

At long, long last, she faced a truth she had been fighting since that fateful morning of her birthday, when he'd walked into her inn. *She loved Alex D'Amour.* From the first time she'd looked into his strange, silver eyes, she'd known, deep inside, that this was the man she'd looked for all her life—intelligent, authoritative, and first-class sexy. He could have been her lover, her confidant and her verbal sparring partner.

Only, after that first, split second of revelation, he'd told her the bad news. He planned to take away her inn. So, she'd fought the feeling, denied it with all her strength.

But now, glorying in the torturous sweetness of his lovemaking, she could no longer lie to herself. She loved Alex D'Amour with all her heart and soul.

Yet, what did he feel for her? His whispered vow at the dance sprang to her mind—his promise of seduction—and her heart clenched. Yes, that was all this little romp was to him. A challenge. A victory to be won. Oh, he probably found her attractive enough to crave a quick fling, but that was all. He'd made his feeling about love quite clear.

Ah, yes, love—love to Alex, was selfishness. He might even call this thing he felt, love. But since they both knew his definition of the word, the notion sent a shaft of ice slicing through her heart. It could only verify for her that this act was pure selfishness. A way to satisfy his baser needs while he softened her up for the kill.

As his hands roamed and caressed, making her crazy with desire, a mewling sound of wanting escaped her throat, then a low, desolate sob.

He seemed to sense her turmoil, for he lifted his face to look at her. His eyes glowed, molten, and she lost her ability to speak.

"What's wrong?" His voice was a rough whisper. "Am I hurting you?"

The question stung. There were so many ways he was hurting her. Not the way he thought. Not physically. His body was like heaven, warm, protective, exciting. No, he could never hurt her physically; she knew that in her woman's heart. But emotionally, psychologically, financially. Yes. He was hurting her, and she wasn't sure she would ever recover from the pain.

With great difficulty, she dragged her arms from around him and pressed hard against his chest. "Get off," she pleaded, her voice so fragile she could hardly hear herself.

He watched her, his expression closing in confusion. "What—"

"Get off, Alex," she cried, again, this time with more strength.

He slid sideways just enough for her to wriggle out. After she did, she braced her hands on the snowy ground and pushed up with all her might. When she stood, her legs were buttery, and she felt dizzy as she backed away. "Seducing me won't make it easier to get my property, if that's your scheme," she threatened brokenly, wishing things were different between them. Wishing he didn't have to be her enemy. And most of all, wishing he didn't want anything from her but her love.

He pulled up on one elbow, looking gut-punched. "If your scheme was to turn me into a bent-over cripple—congratulations."

Turning on her heel, she stumbled, righted herself, then scrambled toward the forest and the pathway to the inn.

His raw blasphemy was the last thing Elissa heard before she dashed into the woods.

It seemed like a month before Alex could move. When he finally sat up, he ran both hands through his hair, scattering snow and curses. "What the hell…" He eyed heaven with disgust. "The woman should wear a sign—Hazardous To A Man's Health."

With a long, low exhale he stood, then spied the sled, coated with a new frosting of white. Stooping, he grabbed it and shoved it under one arm. "Damn woman," he grumbled. "I don't know why you waste your time kneeing men. If you really want to disable one, just kiss him like you mean it. Then leave him there to rot."

He started toward the woodland path, stopping after only a few steps. He felt vacant, forlorn, and oddly directionless. Dumping the sled to the snow, he sat on it, resting his elbows on his knees. Staring off into space, he ignored the snowflakes that were leaving cool kisses along the back of his neck and drifting down inside his collar.

He was in trouble.

He wanted this woman. He hadn't wanted any woman this badly since...

He cursed and held his head in his hands. Hell, he'd *never* wanted a woman this badly. He sucked in a cold draught of air, and another, trying to clear his mind, get his head on straight. This lapse into morose introspection wasn't like him. But he couldn't seem to shake the mood. He felt as if sections of his body had been ripped away, and he would never be whole again.

Damn the woman. Damn her silky red hair and her sexy emerald eyes. Damn her smell—so sultry and musky it drove him nuts, even from across a room.

And damn her kisses to hell...

At the memory, pain burned in his belly, and he groaned. It was a good thing he was taking away her inn. If she didn't hate his guts the way she did, things could get out of hand between them. He might grow to love her. Then, maybe, he'd start to comprehend how his parents' passion for each other had made them so unforgivably selfish. That was a place he didn't plan to go.

"Damnation, Elissa Gardenia Crosby..." he growled, then stopped himself. This wasn't her fault. The woman had treated him as if he were a pariah from the moment they'd met. Anything bothering him was his fault. He'd wanted her to kiss him as if she meant it and he'd maneuvered her into doing just that. Shaking his head sadly, he grasped the meaning of the saying, "Be careful what you wish for, you might get it."

He'd gotten what he'd wished for, and now he had himself a truckload of grief. He refused to use the word love, hostile to everything it represented in his life. The *last* thing he wanted to do was experience an emotion that could be so destructive.

"Hate me, Elissa," he muttered. "I *need* you to hate me."

New Year's Eve began badly for Elissa. Jack invited the family to eat at his restaurant, Gallagher's Bistro. Of course, it wasn't the invitation to dinner that unsettled Elissa. She loved the place. It was the fact that Alex had been included. As the only single man and woman in the group, the process of elimination threw them together.

Gallagher's Bistro was a charming place, and as soon as Elissa walked in, she made herself concentrate on the eclectic atmosphere and the aroma of wonderful food. The decor was an inventive mix of dining-room suites, collected from across the country and in Europe. Clever partitions made from brick, stone or beams were constructed in such a way that gave the feeling that each table was in a dining room, all its own.

Settings ranged from Early American, with bandanna's for placemats, to Louis Quarze French, complete with lace tablecloths. A diverse array of light fixtures hung from the ceiling over each table, matching that particular decor—from sparkling crystal chandeliers to simple turned wood and wrought iron.

Though the bistro had a private room for special parties, Jack didn't want to separate his guests from the general gaiety and clamor of other New Year's Eve diners. So, they were shown to a lovely eighteenth Century Colonial alcove with a spectacular view of the valley behind the restaurant. Christmas lights twinkled in the distance, amid the thick-forested hillside. Snowy fir trees glistened like looming spirits in the almost moonless night.

At the head and foot of an unadorned pine table stood ladder-back chairs. Two discarded church pews served as side seating, the rich patina of old wood elegant in its simplicity. The polished floorboards sported a simple red-and-white checkered rug.

A bouquet of straw flowers in an earthenware bowl served as their centerpiece. And a tin lantern with star-shaped holes hung over the table. Its subdued light intensified the mood that they were in a bygone century.

As Elissa entered the partitioned area, she sidestepped and back-stepped, trying to get away from Alex, as she headed for one of the ladder-back chairs.

She grabbed the nearest one, but Lucy shoved her away, in a rare show of pushiness. The blonde gave her older sister a look that seemed to say, "Don't be silly, you want to sit beside Alex." Though Elissa wanted to shout back, "I'd rather be devoured by Bigfoot!" she decided not to make a spectacle of herself in Jack's restaurant.

Reluctantly Elissa ate her dinner beside Alex, every so often grazing his arm with hers as she cut her fillet or reached for cream for her coffee. He would always—*always*—acknowledge her touch with a glance. Odd, though, he wasn't doing much smiling—at least not at her. Ever since yesterday when he'd returned from sledding, he'd been unusually silent. Though, all through dinner, he chatted and laughed with her sisters and brothers-in-law, he gave her a few strange looks. More like glowers.

That was *fine* with her. The less social contact with him—or any other kind of contact—the better!

Though her brain knew that was best, her body reacted to his nearness as if she were a lovesick ninny. His scent caused an unexpected tremor of desire to race through her, making her delicious fillet stick in her throat. She choked so hard, she feared Alex would have to perform the Heimlich maneuver on her. She waved him away, not wanting his arms around her again, for any reason. Not even to save her life. By sheer force of will, she managed to dislodge the bite just in time. It didn't keep her from feeling like a fool.

Once when his leg brushed hers, she froze, unable to lift her fork the rest of the way to her lips. Though his touch was quickly gone, she was paralyzed with a feminine need for him that terrified her. Trying to quell the pounding of her pulse, she forced her body back into action and made herself eat the green beans, hoping nobody noticed her mental short-circuit.

Checking her watch, she prayed the party would soon end. She didn't know how much longer she could keep from grabbing Alex and dragging him under the table—his selfish motives be damned.

"This lemon meringue pie is wonderful," Lucy said, smiling at her husband. "Do you think the chef would give me the recipe? I've never made a good lemon meringue pie."

Jack grinned at her from the head of the table. "I might be able to convince him—since I know his boss."

Elissa made herself laugh, needing to get her mind off Alex's nearness and onto something else—anything else. "As long as you're asking, get the recipe for this pecan pie, too." She passed Lucy a conspiratorial wink, hoping it looked playful. "For *Lucy*, that is. *I* certainly don't want it. I hate pecan pie, myself." She took a showy bite of her half-eaten dessert. It was delicious, but her stomach had been so tied up in knots all evening, her appetite had suffered. This teasing display was her way of apologizing for picking at her meal. "Awful stuff." She made an impish face. "Just awful!"

Jack grinned at her. "I appreciate your sacrifice, eating it so the rest of my patrons don't have to suffer."

Elissa smirked. "I'm a saint." She loved Jack dearly, and the joking repartee they shared always lifted her spirits.

"St. Elissa?" Jack's chuckle sounded dubious. "The Patron Saint of Gin Rummy cheats?"

"I do *not* cheat!" She said, tossing him a mock frown. "*You* cheat."

"No, I just play better than you."

"Well, playing better than me is against *my* rules."

As the group burst out laughing, the waitress came and refilled their water glasses. Elissa noticed the young woman's hand shook as she served. The poor kid was petrified. She'd probably never expected to actually serve the head of the Gallagher Bistro Corporation. Once the waitress had gone, Jack stood. ''If you'll excuse me, I have some recipes to collect.''

''I'll go with you.'' Lucy reached for her purse. ''I want to visit the ladies room.''

Jack circled the table to help her from her chair. Before Elissa knew it, Helen joined Lucy, and Damien said something about calling the baby-sitter. When Elissa started to get up to go with her sisters, Helen placed a firm hand on her shoulder. ''We'll be back in a few minutes. You entertain Alex.''

They were suddenly alone. A nervous wreck, Elissa stared out the plate-glass window as she took a sip of her water.

''I'm sorry about yesterday afternoon,'' Alex said, startling her so badly she sloshed water on her wool jacket.

She peered at him. ''You should be.'' Her heart thudded so loudly at the reminder the noise almost drowned out her words. ''I've never been so insulted.'' Grabbing her napkin, she swiped at her lapel.

He cocked his head, his eyes narrowing. It was evident that he didn't believe her. They both knew how she'd behaved out there, on her back, in the snow— giving him back as good as she got. The word to describe it was not ''insulted.''

She swallowed, shifting farther away from him.

''Have you heard from your lawyer?''

She stilled. ''No.'' She'd been growing more and more alarmed all day. Why hadn't Dr. Grayson called? She'd left messages on his voice mail for two days. Her mood plummeted to deeper, blacker depths. There was no reason for him to avoid calling, unless—unless.

''Look, Elissa—''

"I know. It's only business. You're not stealing my inn. I've heard it all before." She made herself face him, if for no other reason than to send the message that she wasn't a coward, and to assure him that she had *not* given up hope. "If you don't mind. I'd appreciate it if you'd drop the subject. It's been a nice evening for everyone, and I don't want it spoiled."

He watched her solemnly. His eyes seemed eerily brilliant in the muted light. She transferred her gaze to his chin so she wouldn't be affected by his stare.

His jaw worked and she wondered what was going through his mind. Could he be uneasy about something, too? Unable to stop herself, she lifted her glance to his. A shadow of uncertainty glimmered there, confusing her.

"What's your problem?" she asked, suspicious and hopeful. "Starting to have the guilts?"

"The what?"

"Guilts," she repeated. "You know. About trying to throw me out of *my* inn."

His nostrils flared at her emphasis on *my*. "No," he said, but so softly, she wasn't sure he meant it. "I never feel guilty."

She laughed, a caustic sound foreign to her ears. "That talent must come in handy when you steal a person's livelihood."

He broke eye contact and muttered something.

She frowned. What had he said? The instant he'd spoken, Lucy and Helen came back, their chatter covering his remark. Still, with a terrible suddenness, Elissa knew in her heart, and she shuddered, experiencing an absurd sense of loss.

He'd said, "Good, Elissa—hate me."

CHAPTER TEN

Missy, don't plan on having no happy new year. You ain't gonna have one.

THE LAST THREATENING letter Elissa received kept popping into her mind. It seemed to be so long ago, and so far removed from reality, she wouldn't allow herself to worry about it. This was New Year's Eve, a time to celebrate. Even though Alex had been with her every second, she'd managed to have fun at dinner.

The rest of the evening the family enjoyed the inn's fireplace and warm conversation. A vague odor from the recent fire lingered in the parlor, and the boarded-up window reminded them of the near tragedy. Yet, the fact that they were all well, and together, was enough to put the recent emergency from their minds.

Hirk and Jule Boggs baby-sat the twins while the others had been out to dinner. Jule had insisted that Milhouse, their two-year-old, loved the company. So, the Boggs family had been invited to stay for the remainder of the evening to ring in the New Year, as if they were one big, happy family—except for Alex, Elissa's emotional albatross. Even so, she managed to ignore him most of the time. Interestingly he looked at her less frequently that evening, and when their eyes did meet, he dragged his gaze away as readily as she.

She supposed it was because, when he'd discovered he couldn't seduce her, his male pride had been hurt. A smug sense of satisfaction outweighed her depression for a moment. She had a feeling Alex didn't experience failure often, and was happy to give him a big, bitter gulp. Forcing the memory of his kiss from her mind, she tried to catch the thread of conversation.

Lucy's laughter drew her gaze to the couch where she, Jack and Jule were sitting. Hirk stood behind his wife, his hands placed lovingly on her shoulders. "Oh, Helen and Elissa, did I tell you I heard from Stadler?"

"My favorite subject," Jack muttered.

Lucy took her husband's hand and squeezed. "He sent us an early Christmas card."

"The man sent you a Christmas card?" Damien asked from the chair opposite Elissa. His chuckle was disbelieving. "He's such an ass."

Jack grinned. "And he keeps proving it over and over."

"What's he doing these days?" Helen sat cross-legged on the rug beside Damien's chair. Milhouse, Gilly and Glory were huddled in a cluster before the fire, giggling and coloring in Christmas coloring books. "Did he marry that little Sareena?"

"No." Lucy shook her head. "It seems she got smart at the last minute. But Stadler *is* married. To the daughter of the president of Hillside College, in Joplin. And by coincidence, Stadler is now the director of the drama department there." The note of mockery in her voice was evident. "From his note, I don't think he's very happy. It seems that the new Mrs. Stadler Tinsley leads him around by the nose."

"That's good enough for him." Jack entwined his fingers with his wife's. "The way he treated you, Luce, he deserves to live under a woman's thumb."

"Karma." Helen nodded. "I think he's learned to regret dumping our Lucy."

"Somebody dumped Lucy?" Alex asked, dubious.

Elissa glanced at him as he lounged against the mantel, looking tall and sexy in black trousers and a matching cashmere pullover. He glanced from Lucy to Jack. "This Stadler guy sounds like the world's prize fool."

Jack grinned, lifting his wife's hand and kissing her knuckles. "Thank goodness for fools."

"Someday, I'm going to have to hear the whole story that goes with that remark." Alex's grin was directed at the couple; unfortunately Elissa felt its effect—searing through her body like wildfire.

Angry with herself, she tugged her gaze away. As she did, she noticed the mantel clock. Abruptly she stood, relieved to have something to do. "It's almost midnight. Time we started making some noise." She passed a completely disinterested look toward Alex—at least she wished it were completely disinterested—and noticed his grimace of curiosity. His handsome face was stirring even in a scowl, making her heart tumble over itself at the sight. She whirled away, heading for the parlor door. "Pots and pans, everybody, the New Year awaits!"

While Elissa, Jule and Jack grabbed kitchen utensils, Helen, Damien and Hirk bundled up the children.

"What's going on?" Alex asked as Elissa breezed by him toward the front of the inn.

She thrust a wire whisk and metal colander, in his direction. "We're ringing in the new year. Join us if you must."

He turned the wire whisk in his hand, as though he'd never seen one before. "I'm afraid to ask what you expect me to do with this."

She fought a contrary grin at his doubtful tone. "I thought you were never afraid, Mr. D'Amour."

He muttered something that sounded like, "You've changed all that," but Elissa wasn't sticking around to get him to repeat himself. She didn't like being drawn to him, and wanted the feeling to go away.

Trying not to care if he followed her or if he dropped through a hole in the earth, she hurried outside to the front porch. Squatting beside Glory, she placed a saucepan on the floorboards and handed her a wooden spoon. "Okay, sweetie, you bang on that as loud as you can and shout, 'Happy New Year'."

Glory lifted her spoon to start, but Elissa caught it, laughing. "Wait until your daddy says to." She let go. "Okay?"

"'kay." Glory bobbed her head, her eyes big and expectant.

Jack had given Milhouse a pot almost as tall as he, and a plastic spatula. "Okay, champ. Get ready."

Milhouse turned huge, brown eyes up to the adults, his expression as serious as a doctor just before open heart surgery. Elissa had to smile at the child. Though she felt partial to her nieces, she had to admit that Milhouse was a good-looking, bright little boy. She hoped her nieces would grow up to know him well. She had a feeling he would be special in their lives.

Elissa heard jingling and noticed that Gilly held two sets of measuring spoons. Apparently unable to wait, she waved them around, making a delicate noise, giggling delightedly with the new game.

"Okay, everybody." Damien drew her attention. "Let's count it down. Ten, nine..."

As Elissa joined in, holding her soup pan and ice-cream scoop high, she couldn't help but surreptitiously seek out Alex's location. He lounged against a nearby porch support, watching Gilly's solo on the measuring spoons. She was startled to note that he held the wire whisk and colander up, poised for action. It had never occurred to her that he might actually join in the celebration.

"Seven, six, five…"

She felt an electric sparkle dance through her at the sight as he grinned at Gilly, jingling and dancing around like a tiny, winter nymph.

His eyes shone in the reflected porch light, his deep chuckle rich with vitality. There was an energy, an air of enjoying life, about him that bothered her. She didn't want to see that side of him, a side the woman in her longed to know, to touch, to kiss, to love…

"Three, two, one…*Happy New Year!*" everyone shouted, banging and hooting to the high heavens.

As the cacophony intensified, Elissa saw a pint-size body flash by in front of her. She looked down in time to see Gilly run to Alex and grab his trouserleg. Her spoons were nowhere to be seen, and she was sobbing, her eyes wide with fright. It was clear she had no idea that her little jangling recital would escalate into a deafening, scary experience.

Elissa made a move to reach the child, halting in midstride when Alex gave her a quelling look. Laying aside his utensils, he scooped the wailing twin into his arms.

The noise died down, for only Milhouse and Glory were still at it, unaware that Gilly was upset. In a high-pitched, shuddery sob, she cried, "Unka Alex! 'fraid! Unka Alex! 'fraid!" Curling her chubby arms around his neck, she buried her face against his throat, her crying muffled in the thickness of his parka.

"Oh, dear," Helen said, "I didn't think…"

She started toward her daughter, but Damien took her arm. "No, let's go on and celebrate. Alex is doing fine, and Gilly needs to learn a little noise isn't going to hurt her."

Elissa watched Alex as he held the child, patting her back, crooning to her. He certainly seemed more comfortable with toddlers than he had a week ago. The others began to bang their implements again, only with less abandon, in deference to Gilly's fears.

After a minute, Elissa watched as the twin lifted her face away from Alex's throat and stared at him. Her eyes swam with tears. He grinned at her and said something too softly for Elissa to hear. Gilly nodded, her death grip on his neck easing.

At last, to Elissa's amazement, Gilly allowed herself to be lowered to the floor. Alex kneeled beside her and held out the wire whisk. When she took it, he picked up the colander and nodded, obviously giving her the signal to hit it. She did, tentatively at first. Then, when Alex said more loudly, "Happy New Year, Gilly." She grinned, and gave the colander a good whack.

After a few more solid blows, Gilly turned to grin up at her mother and dad. She continued to whack the strainer and started shouting nonsensical things, just to make noise.

Elissa found herself smiling and renewing her efforts at ringing in the new year with raucous enthusiasm. She banged her frustrations out on that poor soup pan until the ice-cream scoop handle broke off, sending the metal scoop flying into the snow.

"Well, Elissa," Jack said, chuckling as the noise died away, "working out our hostilities, are we?"

She was experiencing a bizarre variety of emotions, but no matter how disconcerted she felt, Jack always rated a smile. "I was pretending it was your head, smarty-pants."

"On that charming note, I think we should go inside,"

Helen said with a laugh. "Somebody start a pot of decaf while Damien and I get the girls to bed."

"Wait a minute," Jack said. "I'm not moving until I get my New Year's Kiss."

"I thought you'd never ask." Lucy smiled and went into his arms.

As they kissed, Elissa diverted her gaze, only to catch Damien taking his wife against him, kissing her possessively. Biting her lip, Elissa shifted to look out at the night. The clear, black sky was a striking backdrop for a golden sliver of moon.

She heard a throat being cleared nearby and feared it *wasn't* Hirk Boggs. He was no doubt kissing Jule not far away. Unable to help it, she glanced at Alex. He watched her with a brow raised. His eyes glittered, but his expression gave away nothing of his thoughts.

She tried to assess his features. Was he as uncomfortable being one half of the only couple out here not kissing? Despite his closed expression, she sensed heat in him, a heat he was willing her to feel. What did he think he was, a hypnotist? Did he think she would rush into his arms if he wanted her to? Or was her own longing tricking her into thinking she saw desire in his eyes?

She swallowed hard, wishing she weren't the only Crosby sister who didn't have a love of her own, someone to drag her into his arms and sweep her away to paradise with his hot, lusty love. But if Alex D'Amour thought he would ever kiss her again, he was loonier than—than—well, than she'd been when she'd *let* him kiss her out there in the snow.

Shifting away, she squatted down. "Okay, who's going to kiss Aunt Elissa, Happy New Year?" Her voice was strangely squeaky, and she cleared her throat, as Gilly and Glory rushed at her. But Milhouse won, grasping her by the neck and planting a juicy, baby kiss on her nose. She laughed, kissing him back. "Well, well, it looks like I have myself a new boyfriend." Patting his rosy cheek, she accepted hugs and kisses from her nieces, and her mood lifted.

Rallying the children, she got them to gather up their utensils and herded them to the kitchen. After the squealing toddlers had done their chore, the others came back inside. Hirk and Jule hugged everybody good-night and left for home with Milhouse. Damien and Helen took the girls upstairs to tuck them into bed, while Lucy and Jack prepared coffee and sandwiches.

Elissa gathered up dirty cups and plates from the den. On one last trip to check for dishes, she felt Alex's presence. Turning around, she feigned nonchalance, but her pulse doubled its beat. "What?"

His grin was melancholy. "I wanted to wish you a Happy New Year." He shrugged. "Now that we're into the new year, I guess you were right. The letters were a hoax. I'm glad."

Stunned by his declaration, she hardly knew how to respond. It was curious, though, that the mere suggestion that he believed the letters to be a hoax lifted a great weight off her. Only now did she face how frightened she had been—how she'd been on edge all evening.

She inhaled in an effort to look serene. "Apology accepted." Her quick scanning of the room was due to nervousness at his quiet nearness rather than to any assumption that she'd missed a dish.

He seemed to hesitate, and she couldn't imagine what he was thinking. He didn't seem any more comfortable to be standing there than she. Needing to fill the awkward quiet, she asked, "Something else?"

He stood practically beneath the mistletoe, looking

painfully handsome. The solid outline of his chest and shoulders strained against his cashmere sweater. She remembered the hard, manly feel of his body as she lay beneath him in the snow. A suffocating sensation tightened her throat as she fought a craving to run to him, to fling her arms around those wide shoulders and kiss him until they both burst into flames.

"I—" He stopped, his lips closing in a firm line. "Nothing—Happy New Year, Elissa."

He turned to go, but something inside her couldn't let that happen. "Alex—wait…"

He shifted to look back.

Now it was her turn to shrug. She scrambled for something to say. "I—just wanted to thank you for being so nice to Gilly."

One corner of his mouth turned up. "Did you expect me to kick her down the steps?"

She felt foolish and lowered her gaze to his boots.

His chuckle was scarcely more than a derisive grunt. "I'm gratified to see you continue to hold me in such high regard."

When her gaze shot to his eyes, she thought she saw angry lightning, but before she could ponder why he might be upset, the phone rang, jarring her.

Glad for a reprieve, she edged past him to reach for the wall phone behind the reception desk. She didn't care who was calling at twelve-thirty in the morning on New Year's Day. Any distraction was better than standing there, fighting her longing for a man she couldn't have—shouldn't want.

"Hello?" She was startled at how breathless she sounded.

"It's Jule, Miss Elissa."

She smiled into the receiver. "Hello, Jule. Forget something?"

"Sure did." The woman's strong voice barked out a laugh. "Forgot to tell you a package arrived after you all left for dinner. I put it on your desk. I'm sorry, but we was having such a good time, it slipped right outa my mind."

"Oh?" Something heavy and hot dropped into Elissa's stomach. "No problem," she murmured, trying to keep sudden misgivings from her voice. "Thanks for calling."

"My pleasure. Now you all have a Happy New Year, ya' hear?"

"You, too…"

Elissa sucked in a nervous breath as she hung up.

"Hey, you two, sandwiches and coffee are ready," Lucy called from the kitchen.

Damien and Helen were coming down the staircase. "Music to my ears," Helen said. "I'm starving."

Elissa waved, manufacturing a smile. "Me, too." She didn't know why, but she had a sick feeling that the package in her office spelled disaster.

"Elissa?" Alex sounded cautious. "Is everything all right?"

"Sure." She waved him off. *A package?* her mind cried. The threatening letters loomed again in her brain. What if it were… She fought down panic. It couldn't be! It couldn't be a bomb!

"Elissa, are you coming?"

She realized Alex had moved ahead of her and turned back when she didn't move.

"Of course." With a quick, fake smile, she ambled toward the basement, compelling herself not to run. "I need to check something, first. I'll only be a minute."

Once she'd strolled halfway down the steps, Alex had gone into the kitchen, so she flew the rest of the way. Tearing around the corner into her office, she spied the thick Federal Express envelope. Scared to death, she crept to the desk, scanning it. Her gaze caught on the return address.

Dr. Grayson!

One fear vanished as another billowed in its place. It wasn't a bomb, at least not one that could maim or kill. But the information in this envelope could be every bit as explosive—at least to Elissa's life. Like a booby trap, it lay there, the truth about who owned her inn lurking inside.

Fingers trembling, she tore open the package and dumped the contents on her desk. The documents she'd given her law professor lay there. But why had he sent them back without a word? Why hadn't he called?

Shuffling through them, she found a sheet of plain stationery containing a handwritten note. She immediately recognized the bold scrawl of Dr. Grayson, though the script seemed less confident, even a bit unsteady. Confused and growing alarmed, she picked up the handwritten letter. It began:

My dear Elissa,

This is not the way I would have preferred to hand over this information to you. However I was in a car accident on the twenty-eighth, and have been in the hospital with a concussion and broken jaw. It wasn't until today that I was allowed visitors and my assistant brought me the final results of your legal problems. I am sorry to have to report that I have determined that the property undoubtedly belongs to Mr. D'Amour.

Sinking to her chair, Elissa forced herself to read on.

I am distressed beyond words about the outcome, and if I were able, I would have traveled up there to be with you to soften the blow and to give you support during this unhappy time.

I wish there were something I could do to ease your mind and heart. You know that I think of you as a daughter. So if you need anything—money or a place to stay—please don't hesitate to call on me.

Oh, concerning my condition, please don't worry. You know I am too hardheaded to really be hurt. A few more days in the hospital and I shall be able to go home to recuperate. I will call you as soon as I'm able.

Take care of yourself, and remain strong, my dear,
Gregory Grayson

"No..." Ice spread through her veins as she reread the dire words. She took in a shuddery breath, her grief a steel weight on her soul. The inn wasn't hers. It belonged to Alex D'Amour, after all.

A raw, primal grief overwhelmed her, and she crushed the letter between her fists. A sob escaped her throat. *"No—no—no..."* she cried, dropping her face to the pages and pounding the desktop in macabre cadence, keening denials issuing up from the depths of her being. *"No—no—no..."*

She didn't care that her tears flowed over the papers that proved she'd been swindled, and that because of her, her sisters had been swindled, too. The inheritance their father had worked hard to earn, to set aside for his daughters' well-being, that inheritance the Crosby sisters had pooled so that Elissa could fulfill her dream—was gone. Like a flower petal, plucked and released in the wind without thought or care. Gone.

Everything—gone.

She was a stupid fool. An incompetent, ignorant idiot who didn't deserve the love and trust her family gave her. How could she have been so—so inept? Elissa Gardenia Crosby, the eldest, strong, competent sister who could handle anything all by herself, had proven to be nothing but a con man's sucker.

Wretched, she swallowed against the hot, sour taste of defeat burning her throat. The last threatening letter came back to her.

Missy, don't plan on having no hapy new year. You ain't gonna have one.

She choked out a despairing laugh that became a low, wailing sob. Alex might not have written the letter, but he certainly made it true.

"Elissa?" Alex's voice was hushed, troubled. "My God, what's wrong?"

She squeezed her eyes shut. "Go away."

A hand on her shoulder made her start. "What is it? What's happened?"

She drew up on one elbow, running a trembly hand through her hair. "I'm all right." She swiped at tears with the heel of her hand, then peered at him. "Don't you know how to knock?"

He was holding a plate containing a sandwich. His expression grim, he set the dish aside. "Is it another threat?"

She shook her head, looking away. "No—more like—

a promise—'' Her voice broke. Struggling to regain her poise, she pushed herself up, shoving a tuft of curls out of her face. "The inn is yours, Alex." She gave him one brief glance, her expression controlled, though her cheeks were wet with tears. "Congratulations." She fought to keep her anguish from shattering her dignified facade. "If you'll excuse me, I'd like to be alone."

She walked stiff-backed from her office and was relieved that she couldn't hear his footsteps following her. No doubt he was looking over the papers. Being a thorough man, he would find Dr. Grayson's letter, though it was torn and wadded.

When she reached the top of the basement steps, she turned away from the kitchen, where she could hear her sisters and brothers-in-law laughing and talking. Retrieving her coat from the staircase hall, she went outside onto the porch and gulped the crisp, cold air, trying to bolster herself. She felt so lost, alone and broken.

With no destination in mind, and no reason to care where she went, Elissa trudged down the steps. Her ankle boots protected her feet from the snow, but she hardly noticed. She was so beaten down by the news, worrying about anything so trivial as catching a cold barely penetrated.

The stillness and the quiet welcomed her; the blackness of the night seemed like an embracing friend. In a daze, she walked toward the darkness, toward the silent wood, not wanting to think. For to think would bring such crushing awareness and culpability down upon her, she wasn't sure she could stand it. At least not now. Now, she needed to be alone. To be still. To walk the land she had grown to love.

She needed to be able to say goodbye—alone—before she broke the news to her family. She had no choice, this time. They would have to be told. But not now. She would wait until after they'd gone, and write to them. To spare them until the end of their vacation. A few more days would make little difference.

She heard a sound, a crunch of snow, and she frowned. Why must he follow her everywhere? Why couldn't he leave her to her sorrow? Did he have to witness her suffering? Did he get some kind of sick jollies out of watching her grieve?

Twirling, she hissed, "You've taken enough from me. Must you take my privacy—" She stopped short.

Cocking her head, she tried to get a better look at the figure rounding a large spruce. Uncertainty nagged at her. "Why, you aren't—" Before she could finish, he lunged for her. A rough hand clamped down over her mouth and nose, cutting off both her words and her air.

"Well, well, missy..." her attacker whispered, his voice gravelly, his breath rank with whiskey. "I been waitin' for this."

CHAPTER ELEVEN

ALEX didn't feel a sense of victory, only a hollowness as he scanned the legal papers scattered over Elissa's desk. Her tears had left the top page wet and puckered. Not sure why, he laid his palm over the dampened paper. An unexpected and disturbing feeling went through him at the touch, a ferocity of passion that he had never experienced, until now.

He was angry with himself for making her cry. He knew her well enough to realize she wasn't a woman who broke down easily, yet he had managed to drive her to tears. The page beneath his palm began to burn where only seconds before he'd felt cool moisture. A preposterous guilt tore at him, and he crumpled the piece of paper in his fist. With a dark curse, he threw it against a wall, damning himself for caring.

Less than three weeks ago, Elissa Crosby had been nothing more to him than a name. He'd come here with a legal claim on the property she thought was hers, and he had known he was within his rights to do so. Her problems had been no concern of his.

But now, his responsibility for her sadness ate at him. It shouldn't. He must *not* let it. With gritty determination, he cast the memory of her haunted expression from his mind. He'd known how this would come out from the moment she'd told him she would fight his claim. He'd known she would lose. So what was his problem?

The word "love" tried to claw its way through his defenses, but he blocked it. He didn't love Elissa Crosby.

What he felt for her was a passing infatuation, a challenge. That was all. Struggling to regain his detached indifference, he left the office and walked up the stairs to the kitchen, his festive mood gone.

Helen shifted in her seat to look over her shoulder at him as he entered. "I thought I saw you and Elissa outside, just a second ago."

Alex shook his head. "No—she went for a walk, but I've been downstairs."

Helen frowned. "Hmm." Turning back, she indicated the side window. "But...I was sure that was you with her, going into the woods." Looking back, she said, "If it wasn't you then who—"

His gut knotting with cold, hard terror, Alex suddenly knew who was with Elissa. *"No! God, no!"* Turning on his heel, he grabbed the kitchen doorknob. "Call the police!" he yelled as he barreled outside.

He came to a halt midway between the inn and the fence. Alerting himself to the slightest sound, he even stopped breathing, trying to detect anything—the crack of a fallen branch, the squeak of snow compacted underfoot. The roar of his blood thundering in his ears was the only sound he could hear. "Damn me," he moaned, scanning the ghostly woods. "I should have done more!"

"What the hell..." Damien came running down the steps, tossing Alex his parka and a flashlight. "What's going on?"

"Elissa's been getting threatening letters." Alex shrugged into the coat. "I'm afraid the bastard who sent them has her."

"Why the hell didn't she say anything?".

Alex looked at him, his frustrated expression saying it all.

Damien's curse hung in the air. "Damn woman and her independence. Then, why didn't *you* tell us?"

"She said it wasn't my business." Eyeing heaven, Alex exhaled, disgusted with himself. "I guess I wanted to believe that." Turning away, he trudged deeper into the darkness. "We have to find her. Look for tracks."

Just as Alex reached the fence, he spotted what looked like the trail. Two sets of footprints; one appeared as though the person had been half dragged.

"Over here," he shouted, waving his flashlight.

Jack bolted out the door, shouting, "The police are on their way." Both he and Damien jogged toward Alex as he leapt the fence. Running into the dense woods, he following the dim trail, getting a head start on the other men.

"Help!"

He veered toward the sound. "Elissa?" Dodging and ducking, he crashed through the forest, evergreen branches stinging his face as he ran. "Are you okay?"

"Alex! Alex!"

She was gasping and sounded terrified. He couldn't tell from her voice if she was hurt, but he sent up a silent prayer of thanks that she was alive.

Weaving through the damnable undergrowth, he batted back limbs, his flashlight hardly penetrating the tangle of trees and snow-clogged weeds. In the dense wood, every shadow danced and lunged as his light swung and dipped with his mad dash. His heart pounded with dread and self-loathing. One eye began to sting, and he realized a branch had cut his forehead, bloodying his face. Half feeling his way, he charged through the tangle of snow-clogged weeds and branches, tripping and stumbling. "Elissa, are you hurt?"

He could hear Damien and Jack in the distance, but

nothing else. He floundered in a drift, righted himself, then stumbled on like a blind man.

"Alex!" Elissa cried, sounding close by.

He skidded to a halt. Finding himself in a small clearing, he spun around to locate her. What he saw, stunned him. Elissa deftly took her knee to a burly man, who howled and doubled over. Almost faster than Alex could see it happen, Elissa whirled behind the man and rammed her foot into the back of his knee, knocking him into a kneeling position. With a warlike shout, she did some sort of karate chop to the back of his neck or between his shoulder blades, Alex couldn't be sure. This time, the man went all the way down, hard and flat on his face.

By the time he reached Elissa, she stood above her attacker, one foot squarely in the small of his back. Grasping a beefy arm with both fists, she twisted it behind him. The man on the ground moaned in agony.

"Elissa?" Alex asked, breathing hard. He was tensed and ready for battle, but it seemed the battle was over. "Are you okay?"

She smiled. Though the effort was weak, he'd never seen a more beautiful sight. "I bruised my knee, but I think it hurt him more than it did me."

"Get this witch off me!" the man whined, but with another torque on his arm, he yelped, then grew quiet.

Jack and Damien rushed into the clearing. In a flurry of activity, the man on the ground was hustled out, his wrists secured behind him with Jack's belt. Watching the subdued attacker stagger along between the brothers-in-law, it was plain to Alex that he wasn't going to cause anyone else trouble for a good long while. He didn't look as if he felt well, bent over and groaning the way he was.

Alex turned to scan Elissa from head to toe. Her hair was tousled and he had a tremendous urge to brush it back from her eyes. Deciding not to think about it, he simply did it, grinning down at her. "You're dangerous, you know? I think you broke that man's arm."

She slumped against an oak and closed her eyes. "Do you know who that was?"

He grew serious. "No. But he wrote those letters, didn't he?"

She nodded and looked at him, her expression sad. "I've heard about people like him. They're called love-obsessed stalkers. They pick a victim almost randomly—somebody who unknowingly attracts them while shopping or buying gas or whatever."

She shook her head and stared off into the shadows, as though recalling something. "He—he worked behind the counter in the dry cleaner's I used to use. When they ruined a skirt, I complained and changed cleaners. I guess he took that as a personal rejection. I—I didn't connect it, but the first letter came a couple of weeks after I complained."

She lifted her gaze to meet his. "Alex, I don't even know his name." Her lips began to tremble, and he could tell the adrenaline rush was beginning to wear off. "When he was dragging me out here, he told me he started the fire. You were right about that, too—and I was wrong. I—I guess I'm pretty much a failure at everything…"

"A failure?" he echoed dubiously. "After what you did tonight, how can you say that?" He reached out to take her into his arms, not caring about anything but comforting her.

She saw his intent and something like fear flashing in her eyes. "No…" She stiff-armed him, her fingers splayed against his chest. "Don't patronize me, Alex. Don't pity me, and *please* don't touch me." Her voice was shaky, but uncompromising. "I appreciate your help, but I think you know we have nothing to say to each other."

Tension stretched between them as their gazes clashed. Her hand pressing against his chest became the only thing in his world, his entire reality. One small force of will, commanding him to stay away. His heart cried out to brush her arm aside, to drag her against him and kiss away her fears. But when he looked deeply into her eyes, all he saw was reproach for him—and for herself.

Sirens off in the distance grew louder as the tension in the air between them became palpable. Suddenly Elissa propelled herself from the tree, hurrying away from him. Experiencing an odd mixture of relief and loss, he watched her go, her head held high. This was what she wanted—and what he needed. He'd almost lost control a moment ago, almost allowed himself to admit an emotion for Elissa that he couldn't consider—couldn't deal with—for it was an emotion he mistrusted.

At two-thirty in the morning, the police were gone and the attacker was in custody. Elissa sat at the kitchen table, staring into a cup of cooling coffee, sensing the glowers of her family. She felt like a specimen being examined under a microscope.

Glancing up, she peered around the table. Everyone was seated, except Alex. He stood some distance away, leaning against the wall near the kitchen entrance. He sported a bandage above his right eye. Avoiding his gaze, she lifted her coffee mug to her lips, gratified her hand was no longer shaking. She sipped the tepid brew, then set it down with a thump. "Look, everybody, it turned out okay. I wish you'd forget it."

"Forget it?" Helen's whisper was horrified. Leaning across the table she took Elissa's hand. "The man could have murdered you, honey. Why didn't you think we should know?"

Embarrassed, Elissa pulled her fingers from her sister's grasp. "I didn't want to worry you. It could have been nothing more than a prank."

"I'm not laughing." Jack said. "Look, Lis, you don't have to take on the world by yourself. We're here for you." He squeezed her shoulders. "Remember that."

Her eyes filled, and she swiped at a tear. "Thanks…" She couldn't bear the soft reproof in his gaze, and shifted to look at Helen and Damien. "I know you're all here for me." She made herself smile. "Let—let's all go to bed. Everything's okay."

Alex cleared his throat. Against her will she glanced his way.

He crossed his arms over his chest, his eyes silver slits of disapproval.

She could read the message in his hard gaze. He thought she should tell her family everything—that she didn't own the inn. Gritting her teeth, she balked at the notion. "What is it with you, Alex?" she growled. "Do you thrive on being ejected from homes?"

His crooked grin was almost sad. "My parents helped me become accustomed to rejection. I can handle it."

"What are you two babbling about?" Helen asked.

Elissa ran a hand over her face, silently condemning Alex to whatever hell meddling shyster-lawyers were damned to. "Nothing—nothing…" she muttered. "Everything's fine."

Uneasy with her lie, her glance flitted back to Alex.

He held her gaze in a vise grip, but said nothing. He merely looked at her, almost through her. His steady perusal was unnerving and cruel, making her feel tremendous guilt. "Okay, okay," she moaned, "maybe everything's not *quite* fine."

"What does that mean?" Helen twisted in her chair to look at Alex. "What's going on?"

He pursed his lips and shrugged, his glance remaining on Elissa.

Helen turned back. "What are you keeping from us, Lis?"

Elissa felt sick to her stomach at the concern in her sister's voice. Dragging her gaze from Alex, she mumbled, "There's this *little* problem, er, with the inn..." Her voice caught and she couldn't stand the thought of saying it aloud. Lurching up from the table, she made for the door, but Alex snagged her wrist. "You're doing fine, don't stop now."

She jerked on his hold. He let her go so easily she almost upended herself. Though his touch was gone, her skin still tingled from it, and she registered the loss. *Was she insane? How could her body betray her so with this man, even now!*

Suddenly the decision was entirely hers. She could run, or she could stay and face her family. She could admit her failure, or she could go on hiding it. Whatever she did, she knew that ultimately the truth would have to come out. Her conscience nagged, *Are you being fair to keep on lying and lying? Isn't it better, more honest, to tell them now rather than write them later? What kind of a sniveling chicken are you?* She cringed. Now her own conscience was against her—calling her names. That was too much! One thing Elissa had never been, and that was a coward.

She pulled her lips between her teeth to keep them from trembling. Alex was right. She had to face it. Her family had a right to be involved.

Yet, even knowing all that, she eyed him with resentment before she faced her family. "Okay, here it is in a nutshell. The inn doesn't belong to me. It belongs to Alex. I was tricked by a con artist. The crook was good, but that's no excuse. I've lost everything—your investments, my inn..."

Nausea swept over her, and she had to choke back bile. "Mr. D'Amour is tearing down the inn to make room for his golf course, and I have to be out of here by the end of January. I kept it from you because I was fighting his claim, but tonight I got the bad news." Peering sideways at Alex, she cried brokenly, "Are you happy now?"

Though his face remained solemn, he winked in answer, and she had the most bizarre feeling that he was proud of her.

The room went as quiet as a tomb. Elissa watched her family stare at her.

"Then you and Alex aren't—close?" Helen asked.

"No," Elissa growled. "We pretended to be friends so your vacation wouldn't be ruined."

"Oh—oh, Elissa, I'm—we're so sorry!" Lucy's blue eyes glimmered with tears.

There was a scraping of chair legs, and Elissa caught movement as Jack stood. His expression was closed but not angry. He seemed more unhappy than outraged. "Alex," he said quietly, "I think, under the circumstances, it would be best if you stayed in a hotel until Elissa vacates the property, don't you?"

Elissa peeked at the man beside her as he nodded in acquiescence. "I'll send for my bags." With that, he turned away, but stopped, his glance resting on Elissa's face. "Your family is a gift, Elissa." His smile was rueful. "Don't squander it."

Seconds later, he was gone.

January 5 was a dismal day for Elissa, though the sun shone brightly, melting the snow. She hated watching her family bustle about getting ready to leave. Elissa intended to stay at the inn through January, honoring reservations she'd booked through the end of the month. She had notified the staff of the inn's imminent closing, and their usual happy mood dimmed.

Elissa assured her employees that with Alex opening his resort, there would be places for them all. It galled her to think that her employees would go over to the enemy, but she couldn't let her resentment for Alex stand in the way of their employment.

Both Jule and Bella had come to her privately, insisting they wouldn't apply for work with Alex if it would upset her. She'd assured them she was fine with it. She knew they were loyal enough to her, that if she asked them not to, they would never work for him. But that wouldn't be fair to them, since she didn't know if she would ever open another inn, herself.

"Okay." Jack came up behind her and slung a brotherly arm around her shoulders. "I've contacted my real estate man, and he's going to bring over a list of properties for you to start considering." He kissed her cheek. "There'll be a Crosby Inn in Branson, again. And remember, I get first dibs as an investor."

"Wait a minute," Damien said as he came down the stairs carrying two suitcases. "I'm the man she wants as her partner in this deal." Elissa shifted to face him as he added with a grin, "Aren't I, Red?"

She shook her head at both men. "I don't deserve you two, considering what I did."

Damien put down the bags. "That's true. We're hurt as hell." He walked over and curled a finger under her chin, tilting her face up to deposit a goodbye kiss on her jaw. "Keep us informed. And remember, we'd love to have you visit us for a while. Heaven knows Helen has enough animal projects going on. We can always use warm bodies to help feed something or bathe something or set bones or—"

"You silver-tongued devil," Elissa said with a laugh. "How can I refuse such an exciting offer. I'll just get my veterinarian degree and rush right up."

Helen came in from outside. "I've got the twins strapped in their car seats. Is everybody ready to get this show on the road?"

Damien chuckled. "That reminds me, Elissa. We also have a few nieces who'd love to have their aunt 'Lissa visit."

With deep affection she touched his scarred cheek. "When you put it like that, it's a deal."

"Whatever you need," Lucy added, hugging her sister. "And don't *ever* keep secrets again, do you hear?"

Elissa started at Lucy's stern tone. "Yes, ma'am." She smirked, but when Lucy didn't grin back, she grew serious. "Okay, okay. No secrets."

As the Lords and Gallaghers loaded up the luxury rental car, Elissa felt very fortunate. She was touched by her family's offers of help. Alex had been on target about this, too. Her family didn't need her to be their mother, just their sister. She should have included them earlier. Their loving concern helped blunt her feelings of pain and loss.

It was interesting how Alex D'Amour's name was

never mentioned after he left that night nearly a week ago. Her family had been supportive there, too. Somehow they seemed to understand that she not only needed to have him out of her inn, but also out of her thoughts. She wondered if her sisters suspected that she hadn't been able to scrub him from her heart.

She flinched, not wanting to admit the feeling. What did it matter now? He was gone, and with any luck, she wouldn't see him again.

She waved goodbye to her family, managing a real smile. With their help, she would get a new start. If she wanted to open another bed-and-breakfast in Branson, her family would aid her in every way possible. What a relief it was to know she didn't have to depend wholly on herself.

That's what Alex had meant about her family being a gift. She truly had squandered that gift for too many years. Ironically it had been due to Alex's interference into her life—and her heart—that she'd found out what she'd been missing. She'd never felt so free, so unburdened—at least in most areas of her life.

Yet, in one small place, deep in her heart, she was weighted down with a sadness she didn't think she would ever be free of—the heartbreak of foolishly loving the man who took away her dream.

With a bleakness in her soul, Elissa decided to take a walk. Snow fluttered down across the hills and valleys of the Ozarks, a peaceful sight. She loved a soft snowfall, and hoped that ambling in the pure loveliness would lift her spirits.

It was January 31 and the inn was officially closed. An hour ago, she bid her small staff a tearful farewell. Suddenly the place had been too quiet to bear.

Tomorrow the movers would come to put her things in storage. With her future so unsure, she had decided to stay with Bella for a couple of weeks so that she could continue to check out properties, then take an extended visit to Helens and Damien's home.

Though her real estate agent had been helpful, showing her a number of excellent locations, Elissa's heart wasn't in the search, and she hadn't been able to make any decisions. She hoped she would become enthusiastic, soon. She needed to get on with her life.

Wandering along a woodland path, she tried to think of nothing more substantial than the dancing snowflakes. It was cold for midafternoon, and the snow was fluttering down at a fast clip. At least two inches of pristine whiteness covered the land and adorned the winter boughs. The Ozark mountains were enchanting in every season, but her favorite was deep winter. She took a long, slow turn around, gazing at the undulating landscape. Then she stopped. Where was she?

It came to her in a flash. The sledding hill—on Alex's property. With a spasmodic swallow, she made another slow turn, her mind drifting back to the last time it had snowed. To the time she had lain on her back, beneath Alex, kissing him with all the unbridled passion in her soul.

"Oh dear…" she breathed, reliving with painful clarity, the wonder of Alex's lovemaking. How could it be that her longing for him hadn't dimmed one iota? "You *fool*," she cried.

"Did you say something to me?"

Astonished to hear a human voice—especially *that* voice—she almost fell as she spun around. Searching the white expanse, she saw movement as Alex strode into her line of vision from behind the lofty oak at the top of the rise.

Shocked by the impact of his appearance, she froze. He was so compelling, his magnetism so powerful, the mere sight of him was an erotic adventure. Light-headed, she inhaled to regain herself.

Though too far away to feel the heat of his body, she still found herself suddenly warm. Her rational mind told her to turn and run, but her love for him held her to the spot.

He began to walk her way, and she stopped breathing, her gaze gobbling him up. In his parka, jeans and work boots, he strode down the hillside like the conqueror he was. Plunging his hands into his coat pockets, he scanned her, his eyes assessing.

When he was within three feet, he came to a halt, his features enigmatic. "Were you?" he asked.

Confused, she frowned. "What?" Her mind had gone to mush, and now that she could detect his aftershave, she was afraid she wasn't going to get much more lucid.

"Didn't you call me a fool?"

She remembered and her cheeks burned. "I was talking to myself," she blurted, then wished she could cut out her tongue.

His lips quirked.

Defensively she sputtered, "I, er, people have a *right* to—it doesn't mean you're crazy if you talk to yourself!"

"I hope not." His grin was wry. "I've been doing it a lot lately."

That melancholy smile did horrible things to her insides and she gulped. She knew she should hate this man, and she had tried! *Hard!* But she couldn't seem to find it in her. Looking at him standing there, so tall and powerful, yet somehow vulnerable, she had to blink several times to hold back forlorn tears.

"Don't you want to know why I've been talking to myself?" he asked, his features serious.

Unable to trust her voice, she shook her head, wishing she really didn't want to know.

He dropped his gaze to the snow, looking strangely defeated. The uncharacteristic stance touched something inside her. And even though he was responsible for her current plight, she felt a need to thank him for the important lesson he'd forced her to learn. "About my family," she murmured, "you were right, and I owe you for that. Thank you."

When he lifted his gaze to hers again, she was stunned at what she saw. His magnificent eyes shimmered with emotion. "I know that was hard for you, but it means a lot to me that you said it."

She felt a blow to her heart for the little boy who had never known the gift of a loving family. With difficulty, she squashed it. This was the end of their brief relationship, and she needed to cut the bond she felt for him before she did something stupid. Not knowing what else to say, she took a step away. "Goodbye, Alex, I hope—"

"You can have your inn, Elissa."

She stumbled to a halt and stared, positive she hadn't heard him right.

His features grave, he added, "I'll draw up the papers."

He turned to go, and had taken several paces before she found her voice. "But—but *why?*"

With no more answer than the shake of his head, he kept trudging away from her.

Unable to believe he meant it, she ran after him, grabbing his wrist. "I—I can't accept this!"

When he turned his gaze on her, it was intense and sad. "You're backsliding. I thought you'd learned to accept help."

"From my family! People who love me!"

"I love you, Elissa." His tone was so solemn it sounded like an apology.

Her lips formed a stunned "oh" as his declaration echoed in her brain.

I love you, Elissa. I love you, Elissa. I love you, Elissa.

She shook her head to clear the mental fog. "What?" she breathed in a whisper.

He swallowed, looking charmingly defenseless, for the first time not in control of his world. "I know you hate me, but I needed to say it."

She was so shocked, she couldn't move. Yet his gaze, roving over her face, was so stunningly honest, she knew he spoke the truth.

Alex D'Amour loved her.

"But I thought you didn't believe in—"

"Selfish people make selfish love, Elissa." He tenderly scanned her face. "I'll always regret the way my parents hoarded their love. But after knowing you, I've grown to understand love's power—and I've made my peace with my mother and father."

His smile was brief and sad, but the beauty of it wrapped around her like a warm blanket. "Because of you, I know I could be a different kind of parent. You see, in the last few weeks, I've missed having my sweaters dribbled on by baby girls. I found out I like children, and I want some of my own."

He shook his head, looking miserable and irresistible. "There's just one problem. I need for my children to be—ours.'' His eyes drank her up, rueful and passionate. A knot rose in her throat. She had never seen such tender passion in anyone's gaze before. It was a sight she would cherish forever.

The only physical contact they shared was her hand on his wrist. He hadn't made a move to touch her, though he was declaring his love for her, as well as his desire to be the father of her children. She recalled vividly, the last night they'd seen each other, that she'd angrily told him she didn't want him to touch her. How sweet that he was trying to honor her demand.

Glorying in this new knowledge, a surge of womanly power rushed through her. She released his wrist, and he promptly slipped his hand into his jacket pocket. She sensed that he was doing it to keep from taking her into his arms. Joy, hot and heady, bubbled up inside her, but she hid it, lifting her chin a notch. '' Is this your idea of a marriage proposal, Mr. D'Amour?''

The tensing of his jaw displayed deep frustration as raw emotion glittered in his eyes. ''It would be if I thought you'd accept.''

At that instant, she was blissfully happy, wholly alive. Alex loved her! The time for playing coy games was over. Why waste another precious second? She threw her arms around his neck.

Taken by surprise, with his hands in his pockets, Alex lost his balance and stumbled backward into the snow. He lay there, the breath knocked out of him, staring up at her. ''I didn't see that one coming,'' he gritted. ''Knee me and get it over.''

With a wily smile, she straddled him. ''Don't tell me you're afraid. I thought you were never afraid.''

He frowned, appearing confused by her buoyant tone. ''Elissa, what...''

She bent to within an inch of his face. Grazing his jaw with her lips, she trailed her tongue to his ear.

"This isn't karate, is it," he murmured, a note of wonder edging his voice.

"No…" She nibbled his earlobe. "Have you ever made love in the snow—Mr. D'Amour?"

He groaned, sounding like a man who was having a hard time remaining unaffected. "Elissa, I—"

"Hmm?" She teased his ear with her tongue.

"What are you doing?"

"I'm accepting your proposal, silly man."

He drew slightly away to scan her face, and she relished the widening of those remarkable eyes. "Which proposal?" he asked. "The one about marrying me or making love in the snow?"

"No, no," she said sweetly. "The snow thing was my idea."

He searched her face, his eyes reaching into her thoughts, her heart, and she could tell the instant he grasped how she felt. With a low moan, his arms came around her, and he pulled her against him. "I don't know what happened here, but I think I'm ready for it."

Pressed against him the way she was, she could detect his arousal and her heart thrilled. "Oh, yes," she sighed, "you're definitely ready."

"Does this mean you'll marry me?" he asked huskily.

"I love you, Alex," she whispered, his hot, nibbling kisses driving her wild. "And my answer is yes…"

EPILOGUE

CHRISTMAS was special in the Ozark mountains. This Christmas was especially so. Elissa couldn't believe almost a year had passed since that day Alex proposed. A month later, they had been married. Alex had surprised her by inviting his parents. And they'd surprised Alex by coming. Though their interactions had been somewhat stiff after years of estrangement, Elissa sensed that Alex's parents truly wanted a reconciliation. Perhaps their advancing years had taught them a lesson or two about the joys of family and children.

Because Alex had been immediately and wholeheartededly welcomed into the Crosby family, Elissa knew that one day, he would also find his way back into his own.

This year, once again, the Crosby girls and their growing family were gathered together to celebrate the holiday. Alex and Elissa hosted the event at the remodeled D'Amour mansion, which would open that coming spring as a posh resort.

The twins, Gilly and Glory, weren't the only children to arrive this trip. Jack and Lucy introduced their five-month-old son, Jonathan Crosby Gallagher, to the Ozark mountains. Damien and Helen delighted the rest of the clan with another set of twins. This time boys—three month old Jake and Jerod Lord.

After dinner on Christmas Eve, all the children were finally asleep. The family toured the mansion, but Elissa's mind was preoccupied. She promised herself that after everybody was in bed, she would give Alex his Christmas gift. She would present him with a brand-new cashmere sweater, to announce the impending birth of Baby Alex Junior or Alexandra, due in the fall.

"I can't get over how fabulous this place turned out!" Helen said as she returned to the downstairs parlor. Elissa watched her baby sister gaze around the room. With pride, she glanced around, too. She loved the new decor, so light and airy.

A tinted glaze brought depth to the freshly painted yellow walls and a hand-woven rug brightened the hardwood floor. Wide green bands woven into the rug complemented the many plants Elissa had added. The furniture was large-scale and comfortable in this private wing, reserved for family and friends.

"And to think, I climbed through that window on my twenty-first birthday." Helen pointed to one of two tall, arched windows, now unobscured by heavy velvet drapes. Outside, a light snow drifted silently down, the newly landscaped grounds inspiring awe, even blanketed in white. "It seems like an eternity ago."

Damien took her hand and led her to a linen sofa, embellished with a cheerful fern design. "I'm glad you broke in that night," Damien murmured, hugging her against him. "Without you, where would I be today?"

Helen snuggled into his protective warmth, waving Jack and Lucy into the room. "Damien, my love, you'd be a sad, lonely man with more money, women and leisure time than you'd know what to do with."

He laughed. "What a tragic figure I would have been."

Jack and Lucy sat down in a pair of armchairs across from Helen and Damien. "We owe this place a lot," Lucy murmured, touching Jack's arm with affection.

Elissa stood before the stone fireplace. Relishing the fire's warmth and Alex's sheltering arm around her waist, she met her sister's gaze and grinned.

"Lis?" Lucy asked, "I hope you have a room set aside someplace for single girls to sleep in on their birthdays. Even though you don't believe in the myth, you wouldn't keep other women from giving it a try, would you?"

Elissa hugged Alex to her, wondering if she would ever tire of his scent, his texture, the melting beauty of his smile. "Actually..." She cleared her throat. "There is *one* little thing I've been meaning to tell you all—" She slanted a sheepish look at her husband. "I'm afraid it's about the myth—and it affects you, honey..."

Alex cocked his head. "Really? How?"

She stretched up on tiptoe and kissed his smiling lips. "You won't get mad?"

His silver eyes shone with mischief. "Only if you tell me you slept in the damned place on your birthday, then you came out and kneed me in the groin as a reward for being the first man you saw that day."

Stunned, she backed far enough away to get a good look at his face. "How did you know?"

"I didn't—not really." He dragged her into his loving embrace, his gentle gaze full of devotion. "I only know, darling, that my love for you is mythic in its proportions."

Jack chuckled wickedly, "Get a room before you show it to her."

The rest of the family burst out laughing and Elissa was reminded once again of the joys of a close family. She had so much to be thankful for she hardly knew where to start. That wasn't totally true. She knew where she *intended* to start. Taking her husband by the hand, she tugged him toward the door. "If you folks will excuse us, Alex and I have something—to do."

Noticing her sisters' stunned expressions at her revelation about sleeping in the mansion, she asided, "I'll explain later. Trust me—I'm a believer."

Alex squeezed her fingers, setting sparks of electricity shooting through her. His subtle touch telegraphed delightful lovers' secrets that made her sizzle with need.

Moments later he took her into his capable arms, his touch and his kiss stealing her from the world, as wonderful as it was, and soaring with her to their own private heaven.

When the D'Amour resort opened, Elissa and Alex dedicated one upstairs room to be used by single women on the night of their birthday, when the moon is full. To date, Alex and Elissa have only successes to report.

What became of the little Crosby Inn? Why, Alex kept his promise and gave it to Elissa—as a wedding gift. She now offers free honeymoon lodging for other lucky couples whose unions have been blessed by the enchanting legend.

And to this day, the D'Amour myth lives on...

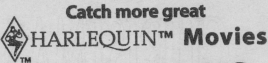

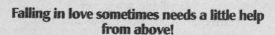
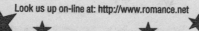

Question: How do you find the red-hot cowboy of your dreams?

Answer: Read on....

Texas Men Wanted! is a brand-new miniseries in Harlequin Romance®.

Meet three very special heroines who are all looking for very special Texas men—their future husbands! They've all signed up with the Yellow Rose Matchmakers. The Yellow Rose guarantees to find any woman her perfect partner....

So for the cutest cowboys in the whole state of Texas, look out for:

HAND-PICKED HUSBAND
by Heather MacAllister in January 1999

BACHELOR AVAILABLE!
by Ruth Jean Dale in February 1999

THE NINE-DOLLAR DADDY
by Day Leclaire in March 1999

Available wherever
Harlequin Romance books are sold.

Makes any time special ™

Look us up on-line at: http://www.romance.net

HRTMW

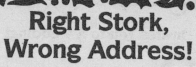

Harlequin Romance®

Invites You to A Wedding!

Whirlwind Weddings
Combines the heady romance of a whirlwind courtship with the excitement of a wedding— strong heroes, feisty heroines and marriages made not so much in heaven as in a hurry!

Some people say you can't hurry love—well, starting in August, look out for another selection of fabulous romances that prove that sometimes you can!

THE MILLION-DOLLAR MARRIAGE by Eva Rutland—
August 1998

BRIDE BY DAY by Rebecca Winters—
September 1998

READY-MADE BRIDE by Janelle Denison—
December 1998

Who says you can't hurry love?

Available wherever Harlequin books are sold.

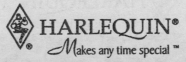
HARLEQUIN®
Makes any time special ™

Looking For More Romance?

Visit Romance.net

Look us up on-line at: http://www.romance.net

**Check in daily for these and
other exciting features:**

**Hot off
the press**

View all
current titles,
and purchase
them on-line.

What do the
stars have in
store for you?

Horoscope

**Hot
deals**

Exclusive offers
available only at
Romance.net

Plus, don't miss our interactive quizzes,
contests and bonus gifts.

PWEB

Coming Next Month

Especially for Christmas we bring you a whole feast of delights.

#3531 READY-MADE BRIDE Janelle Denison

Andrew Fielding wants a mom and his daddy could use a wife. He thinks he's found the perfect woman for both of them: Megan Sanders. Which is fine with Megan—the Fielding men have their attractions: one's as cute as a button, the other's very sexy and, together, they're the family Megan's always wanted! But convincing brooding widower Kane Fielding is less easy....

Whirlwind Weddings—*Who says you can't hurry love?*

#3532 GABRIEL'S MISSION Margaret Way

The way Chloe taunted her boss, Gabriel McGuire, at work could be amusing, but her reckless actions could also be downright exasperating! One of these days she'd take one risk too many. She'd probably worn out a whole host of guardian angels, but some small voice kept telling Gabriel that someone had to protect her and that *he* was the man for the job....

Guardian Angels—*Falling in love sometimes needs a little help from above!*

#3533 ONE NIGHT BEFORE CHRISTMAS Catherine Leigh

When Carly meets Jonah St. John at a Christmas party she decides that all she wants for Christmas this year is the tall, handsome tycoon... gift wrapped! And her wish comes true—at least temporarily. But then Carly learns that Santa's brought her a little something extra this year.... She's having Jonah's baby!

#3534 SANTA'S SPECIAL DELIVERY Val Daniels

Alicia believes that her handsome husband, Daniel, has only married her for their baby's sake, and that he is really in love with another woman. In fact Daniel *is* in love with Alicia, and wants their marriage to last forever—but will he be able to convince her before it's too late...?

Baby Boom—*Because two's company and three (or four or five) is a family!*